THE ASHES OF THE FOREST

ADVANCE READER PRAISE FOR
The Ashes of the Forest

"In a hidden Aegean village where the sea remembers more than the living, a young woman named Azra listens to waves that carry ghosts, stories, and scars. In an idiom that blends lyric with the cadences of folk storytelling and the engagement of ecological writing, *The Ashes of the Forest* unfolds in a world where fragments of myth, from Simurgh to Lilith, are reshaped by the presence of the ghostly sailor Elmados. As the sea returns what cannot be forgotten, the novel magically binds the reader to an endangered natural world."
—ERDAĞ GÖKNAR, Translator of Orhan Pamuk's *My Name is Red*

"Güzide Ertürk's *The Ashes of the Forest* is thoroughly enchanting and captivating. What seems at first to be a Turkish fairy tale becomes an adventure torn from the pages of *The Arabian Nights*, as told by Gabriel Garcia Marquez. Every twist in the story takes you deeper into a magical, watery world you'll be reluctant to leave."
—MICHAEL N. McGREGOR, Author of *The Last Grand Tour,* and *An Island to Myself: The Place of Solitude in an Active Life*

"At once lyrical and imaginative, funny and profound, *The Ashes of the Forest* is an arresting novel full of ghosts and spirits, magic and wisdom. This debut marks the arrival of a singular, innovative new voice."
—GABRIEL URZA, Author of *The Silver State, The White Death: An Illusion* and *All That Followed*

"A marvelously inventive work of fantasy steeped in folklore and magic."
—KIRKUS REVIEW (Starred Review)

The Ashes of the Forest

Güzide Ertürk

Published by Korza Books

The Ashes of the Forest

Contact the publisher by writing to Korza Books at
1819 SW 5th Ave. #293, Portland, Oregon 97201

Published by Korza Books

Original Cover Illustration by Jahongir Ashurov
Cover Design by Yasin Çetin
Author Photograph by Hakan Kutgun
Interior Layout by Olivia M. Hammerman

First English Language Edition

ISBN: 978-1-957024-12-7

Korza Books

To Kerim

"Posidonia Oceanica, the lungs of the Mediterranean Sea, plays an important role in combating climate change. It provides habitat, spawning sites, and breeding grounds for many species. Although this vital species is protected, it faces the risk of extinction due to threats such as boat anchors, pollution, illegal fishing, and urban and industrial waste."

—Turkish Marine Foundation at Tudav.org

CONTENTS

CHAPTER ONE

The Mossy Village

Her Waves

I DIDN'T KNOW WHAT THE sea was going to bring me. Some days she brought me waves and then, a few seconds later, took them back. Some mornings the waves were enormous. They wanted to catch me by my ankle and pull me back with them into the deep water. Some summer days, she would turn into a lake. Her surface was so smooth and clear; I could see her secret pathways in the depths, but it was rare. Most of the time, she sent me her waves traveling along with the wind. The wind sounded like a song, with lyrics that no one could grasp.

Don't tell me all seas are the same. Don't tell me you've also heard the sounds of the wind. Don't tell me the same waves enveloped your feet. It's possible they brought you something; the skull of a dead bird, a giant piece of sea moss, or a flopping fish trying to breathe. Maybe you saw what the waves had for you, or maybe you stepped on it without realizing it. Perhaps you saw thousands of dead jellyfish washed up on the shore, and it was fun to pop them using a branch in your hand. And to watch all the poison they held mix with the sand as they exploded. No, the waves haven't brought me such things.

You have never met my sea. It has never touched you. It will never bring you anything. She lives next to my village, in a secret bay. When she merges with other waters or other beaches, she behaves differently. Her name is Aegean; don't try to understand her. She changes from island to island, bay to bay, inlet to inlet. When you are far from the shore, in the middle of nowhere, you can't recognize her. Her mood can change in the blink of an eye. Aegean never forgives mistakes and can become, in an instant, a furious enemy. Our souls and bodies don't matter to her. Aegean is blind and speechless. With one false step, you will die. If she likes you, she might whisper a legend in your ear but don't expect too much from her.

I learned how to speak with Aegean when I was little. I was familiar with her creatures and small legends, but I never could figure out her silence. It was always sharp. I didn't have a boat and wasn't a captain. No fish ever bit my hook. However, I was a good swimmer. I was a girl from the village, "a peculiar village," other people whispered. It was hard to find it for strangers. Its name has never appeared on a map nor been officially registered in some government document. The carriers of packages were constantly losing their way searching for the entrance, and lost, curious wanderers would occasionally stumble in.

The dense olive groves and fig trees hide our village from the outside world. When the others gossip, they call us peculiar because we don't like talking with outsiders. The sea taught us this over many years. The salt of the sea has adhered to our skin and given it a sheen. On sunny days, my face shines like a fish's scales. Our village's name is only written on a rusty sign half-hidden at its obscure entrance: "The Mossy Village." Next to it, there is another rusty sign but easier to see: "Caution! Dog!" An invisible dog patrols around the village paths. Sometimes we hear its barks, and we know it can bite.

Moss-less

ONE DAY TWO YOUNG WOMEN by chance found us. They were standing right at the entrance. I was sitting out on my balcony, cleaning green beans for cooking, when they saw me and excitedly asked, "Are we close to the sea? Is this 'The Mossy Village?'"

I put down the knife I was holding and with an innocent face, looked up at the sky, feigning to think. After a moment, I lowered my face and said, "I never have heard such a name! There is no moss in our village; look around. It's all sand and stone. It's a long walk to reach the sea. I wish I was that lucky to live next to it. I am afraid somebody has tricked you."

They were so upset and complained, "Do you know how long we have walked! Our feet hurt! Our blisters are bleeding," and I said,

"Do you need some bandages?"

Don't blame me because I didn't tell them the truth. I did those young ladies a favor. The sea's waves would have brought them only trouble and misery. They don't know her language or her mood. When they see the black moss washed up on the shore, when they accidentally step on the urchins covered in needles and injure their feet, even more, they will cry out. They'll want to swim in safer water; moss-less, stone-less, and urchin-less. Before they could step onto clean sand here, a bulldozer would have to scrape off all the mess. I know everyone wants to see what the waves will bring them, but they can't tolerate the unknown.

Figs

I LIVE IN A SMALL, white house behind the entrance sign. A huge fig tree envelopes part of my house with his vast leaves. During the late summer, all the children, squirrels, and bugs come to eat the fruit. And in the early morning, the owls come to eat the squirrels. During the night, the bats come to eat the bugs. The tree is like a central station for the whole village. Everyone loves to stop and rest under his limbs. I like the shadow he casts, and I can spend hours underneath him on the swing hanging from one of his largest branches. Tiny green leaves appear along the fig tree's naked branches at the end of spring. The eldest woman of the village, Sevim, gets upset at me every late May when all the trees start to blossom. Then the pollen from the olive trees starts to fly through the air, and the old shrew likes to amble down the road, basking in it. When I see her, I get goosebumps and ask myself, "Should I hide? What have I done wrong this time?" I want to stop whatever I'm doing and run away someplace, but I always freeze up. It's hard to even move my fingers.

She always mutters, "Don't waste the raw ones this year, will you? Make delicious jam from the raw figs, lazy!" Her small, black eyes always look for something to be upset at. I sometimes fear that they'll pop out of her face and roll down next to my feet like little balls, and her expressions scare me.

However, over the years, I have learned never to show fear to Sevim. I've learned to get up enough courage to shout back so her nearly deaf ears can hear, "It's too early now. Even the leaves haven't finished growing. Why don't you come and pick them up yourself when they are ripe, old lady?" While she shakes her head from left to right slowly, she fixes her scarf. She doesn't notice the few white hairs which sneak out from underneath it. Before she will let me go, she gives one of her long speeches. Everybody knows Sevim's delicious jams and her endless speeches. They're famous around the village.

Somehow, she denies even making fig jams; she expects me to cook them. She says, "You have the most famous and beautiful figs in your garden. It's your job to make the jams, not mine! My hands are tired from picking all the goddamn olives and berries. Nobody helps me! My fingertips are sore. It's not easy carrying the heavy bags by myself. But, when the olives and jams are ready, an endless line appears in front of my door. People love to eat without help." Her talk never ceases. She speaks by making her wrinkled face grimace. She doesn't care about her tired eyes or wrinkles or about taking care of herself. She doesn't complain about the pain in her knees. But she loves her scarves. Every day she wears a different color. When Sevim turns her back and walks away, it seems like she takes all the shadows of the fig tree with her. As if suddenly all the vast leaves of the tree fell to the ground at once and made him naked.

I haven't ever seen her go near the sea. The other villagers told me that she has aquaphobia and that she always turns her back to Aegean. Her hands are always busy picking berries and making jams. She never speaks of the waves. The villagers told me that she saw something in the deepness of the waters when she was a child.

Wounds

ONE DAY, WHEN SHE WAS criticizing me again for not making jams with the dry fruit, I asked her, "Hey Sevim, why don't you come with me to the sea? You are the eldest woman of our village, and I've never seen you swim."

She turned her eyes to the ground like a shy child. For a minute, she forgot about the jams, picking fruit, green and black olives, and murmured, "No, thank you! I prefer to love her from a distance without getting wet."

I insisted, "But it's so hot! The coolness of the water is the best healing for our burning souls."

She just said, "No!" and didn't bother me for a long time afterward.

I don't know what the waves brought her, but I am sure it hurt Sevim. Every villager has a unique scar the sea has given them. Some were tiny, ones that disappeared in a couple of weeks. I have seen some of them. The scars are on their faces, but some are hidden deep inside. They have never healed. It was hard to tell what had caused them, and everyone here knows there is no cure for those.

The scars on my feet would linger for months. By the time I realized I had accidentally stepped on the urchins' stingers, it was already too late. I struggled for days to remove them. They had penetrated deep into my skin, and I couldn't alleviate the persistent ache they caused. One day, I took two small twigs and gathered up a few urchins up onto shore. Hundreds of spines from the bewildered creatures protruded above the water, unsure what to do next. Their wet stems shimmered in the sunlight, making them appear like fireballs rolling across the sand. When I flipped the urchins over, I discovered a small eye. A passerby on the beach remarked that the meat inside the shell tasted delicious, making me feel nauseous. The wounds on my feet tingled slightly. The urchin's lone eye turned toward me and froze in place.

CHAPTER TWO

Elmados Elmuhattel

THE WAVES HAVE BROUGHT ME many other things; some of them were hard to deal with it. One morning, I saw a body on the beach. The black moss covered his whole face, and he wasn't moving. I thought he was dead and was scared to go near him. Should I have called someone, should I have screamed, or should I have turned back and pretended not to have seen anything? I couldn't decide what to do. While I was full of hesitation, his fingers clutched a handful of small pebbles that made up our beach. The gesture washed away my doubts. I walked next to him quickly and, without thinking, threw off all the moss covering his body. It was impossible to find out where the moss ended and where his beard started.

Then I heard a question, "Did we win?"

I answered, "Win what?"

"The battle," he said with a thick voice and coughed, "Yack! The saltwater burns my throat."

I said, "Which battle?"

He opened his eyes wildly and angrily replied, "Guess which one! How many battles have there been lately in this sea? I see some brightness in your eyes. Don't disappoint me. Don't tell me you are so stupid. Don't tell me you haven't heard the sounds of battle in the distance."

I tried to stay calm and took a deep breath before answering. I pointed to the sea with my index finger, "Can you see that horizon? There is an invisible border there. If you reach that place, sailors from the other country will demand you show your identity right there in the middle of the sea. It's a kind of war, but there's never any winner."

He grasped my index finger and held it tight. He grunted, "Don't play with me."

I protested, "Let my finger go!" After having saved my finger, I was able to respond, "I don't know what you are talking about, but it's not hard to guess: You lost! Otherwise, why would you be here, under this black moss? If you had won, the waves wouldn't have brought you here."

He murmured, "We haven't lost. I died in battle."

To which I replied, "Well, that's just great!"

We didn't dare to talk for a long time. The sailor was finally able to get up. All of his clothes were tattered and wet, but he didn't care. I watched him from a distance. Was he really dead? His skin was pale, and his limbs were light pink. These weren't signs of death. His face was very lively, lit with anger and curiosity under his wet hair. He went back into the water knee-deep and started searching for something, bent over with his hands. It was the first time I had seen a glint in his gloomy face. "Oh, here you are!" he said and pulled out of the water a wooden box and dragged it ashore. He was ignoring me now. The sailor opened the box and said, "Wine!" grabbed the bottle in it, and opened it in a hurry. However, when he started to pour, only sand came out. He threw the bottle back into the sea and then kicked the box with a curse. When he had calmed down enough to remember my existence, he turned to me and said, "No, we haven't lost yet."

"The waves will take him back," I thought, "The Mossy Village wasn't a good home for a ghost." The sailor should have gone right back into the deepness of the waters, but he stayed. The waves haven't touched him for a long time.

Win or Lose

THE FOLLOWING DAY, WHILE I was preparing my breakfast on the balcony, I saw him resting under the fig tree. The sailor was staring at the table, waiting for an invitation. He was dry now, and his beard and hair had become curly. His clothes were bleached from the sun and salt. I told you, we don't like outsiders in this village, and the last thing I wanted was a spirit at my table.

The sailor said, "I don't remember the last time I put food in my mouth. It had to be many years ago."

While eating a cherry jam with cheese, I said, "Then you can stay hungry forever."

He said, "The only taste I know is that of salt now! Bloody salt! It's everywhere in my body. On my skin, on my tongue, and in my blood."

While taking a sip from my tea, I said, "Do you still have your wound? Tell me, how did you die."

He noticed the figs above his head and stopped staring at my breakfast. Without even taking off the skin, he popped one of them into his mouth and closed his eyes in joy, "Oh, these are delicious."

I walked over to him and asked, "When will you go back to the sea?"

He was busy with more figs, and without looking at me, he answered, "When you tell me, did we win or not."

I replied, "Why is winning so important to you?"

The sailor started to climb up the branches and responded, "Because then I will rest in peace under the waves if I knew that we won."

I must have asked a thousand questions trying to figure it out. Where was he from? What year was he born? Which battle was it? Who was his captain? Who was he fighting against? "Did you leave anyone behind when you left for battle?"

The only answer I ever got was, "I don't remember. The water has washed away most of my memories. I know the waves, the black moss, and the salt. I know that existing under the sea is so boring. I miss living!"

I also asked him his name.

He said, "Elmados Elmuhattel," and then he added, "Call me Elmados."

The waves forgot about me. They didn't bring me anything for a long time, and they didn't take back Elmados. He started to search around the village with an endless curiosity, to the point that he became a nightmare. Every villager—except me—began to complain about the dreams that they had been having. They were all saying the same thing; a dead sailor was following them around, asking precisely the same question, "Did we win?" The village kids started crying when it was bedtime, and even the babies had trouble sleeping. Sevim took a break from picking her berries for a while. Nobody wanted to swim. Nobody wanted to smile. Everyone was trying to figure out, "Did the ghost's side win?" except me. Elmados didn't intrude on my dreams. He chose to bother me while I was awake. Every morning was the same. I would go out on the balcony and see Elmados waiting under the fig tree.

Fire!

IT WAS A PITCH-DARK NIGHT. I opened my eyes to the darkness with a shout from the outside, "Fire!" In a panic, I jumped up from my bed and ran to the balcony.

It came again, "Fire!"

The first thing that came to my mind was that the orchards were on fire or someone's house, but then I recognized the voice. It was Elmados, wandering around the village like a drunk sleepwalker. I wrapped a blanket around my shoulders and, without thinking, went outside. It was cool and dark, and the stars were twinkling brightly in the sky. A small group of fireflies was dancing in the air under the fig tree. The crickets were chirping incessantly.

I heard him again, "Where is my wine? I said, 'fire!' This lazy crew never listens to me." It was hard to find him in the dark, but I followed the sound and caught up to him next to the sea. He was shouting out to the black waves. His angry eyes shone like flashlights.

Before Elmados could talk, I said, "Hush! Another sleepless night because of you! Do you want a fire? Then pick some driftwood from along the shore. Maybe a campfire would bring you some light."

He stared at me in silence. I felt it was then that he snapped out of it and recognized that he was no longer on his ship. He didn't shout nor even speak.

I picked up some driftwood for him and said, "Don't you dare wake me up in the middle of the night again!"

Elmados remained quiet. As soon as the flames flared up, he lay down by it and drifted off to sleep. However, I couldn't. I hugged my blanket tightly and watched the somber sea without any thought or emotion. I didn't know what to feel. Elmados started to snore. A fishing boat passed close by, traveling along the seashore. Its lights swung with the waves. A few hours later, the sun came up. I was freezing and walked back home. And fell into a dreamless sleep in my warm bed.

The Pearl Seller

I'D HEARD OF THE PEARL Seller before, but I had never met him. There was an old marble wall on the north side of the village, as well as an unspoken rule every villager knew, "Don't go beyond the wall." On it hung a yellow sign with the words "Blind Alley." It wasn't a very tall wall, not higher than my stomach, but it was forbidden to jump to the other side. Nobody had ever told me that in so many words, but I could feel that invisible, forbidden line in my skin from childhood. Beyond the wall seemed terrifying. My friends and I were always afraid of that place. I would quicken my steps when I passed by because of the unusual sounds that came from it: a snake's hiss, the footsteps of a fox, or that of a shadow scraping along its marble stones. The orchids and the thick branches of olive trees clustered along its edge on the other side didn't allow anyone to glimpse much of what was beyond the wall. When I was a young child, yet unafraid, I would tempt fate and run along the top of it. But one day, I fell and broke my ankle. Since then, the old pain returns every time I come near it.

I knew only one truth about what was behind that barrier. In the olive groves lived a pearl seller who used to be a fisherman but had not sailed Aegean since his wife had died. Some claimed, "He found treasure deep beneath the waves." They whisper, "He collected them in secret for many years until his eyesight began to fail, but after his wife's death, he has never gone out to the sea again." Everyone in the Mossy Village called him "The Pearl Seller," but we were never his customers. His patrons came from faraway lands just for him. I'd never seen his face, yet the man was known throughout the world.

I heard that no ear had ever listened to his strange tales. No eyes had ever seen what he had seen under the waves. No one dared to dive as deep as he did. No fingers had touched what he had handled before. So, maybe he could give me some advice on Elmados. Despite the unnatural sounds emanating from the other side of the marble wall, and without thinking about the old pain in my ankle, I jumped over it. Some tiny branches scraped my skin, but it didn't hurt as much as I thought it would. It didn't even bleed. As soon as I stood up on the other side, the frightening sounds ceased. The woods were listening carefully to my unpredictable steps. I eventually found the Pearl Seller's tiny house on the slope of a hill surrounded by olive groves facing the sea. When he opened the door, we stared at each other's faces. I don't know what he saw in mine, but in his, I saw the lines of a skilled fisherman, a pearl seller, and an ordinary old man. There were clouds in his lonely light blue eyes, and I saw melancholy in his short white hair. Suddenly he frowned and became angry.

The merchant said, "You don't have enough money to buy what I have."

I said, "I don't want to buy pearls. I just want to ask you something. If you don't know the answer, I promise you'll never see my face again. Have you ever heard of a sailor called Elmados Elmuhattel?"

He looked at me in silence for a while. Then his face softened, and he smiled, "My old ears have heard many names since I was born. Why don't you come inside?" And he opened the door all the way. His stone house was modest for an affluent pearl seller. The part of the house facing the sea was glass from top to bottom. The view from it was stunning. It was like flying atop Aegean. The foam of the waves formed white streaks, and they were many. I started to feel dizzy.

Then, standing just behind me, the Pearl Seller said, "Tell me, who is this Elmados?"

I answered, "A dead sailor who wants to know whether he won or lost. He talks about a battle he was in many years ago, maybe even millennia before! He ate almost all the figs in my garden." I heard the old man's footsteps as he came up beside me. We watched Aegean in silence. Dozens of seagulls on the rocks watched the sea with us. One of them noticed us and flew next to the window.

After a long silence, the man started to talk. The seagull flew away while we both continued staring at the waves. "I don't know him. What I do know is we are not alone in this inlet. Many people and other creatures have lived here before us, and they've been going on living. One day we'll pass, but this land will stay. It would be best if you accepted his existence. He is injured like the rest of us. It doesn't matter if he lived thousands of years ago or hundreds or only a couple. He has a soul and doesn't know what to do with it. But be careful. Don't forget that he is a ghost." The Pearl Seller paused and breathed deeply. "He came from the sea. The black moss brought him to you." The old man touched his cheek with his finger and made a long line, "He can wound you easily. He can give you a scar that will never heal. Let me make you some tea!"

"He needs to stop asking me about his battle and realize that he's not on his ship anymore!"

He turned his blue eyes towards me; I saw the waves inside them and stated, "He will. But first, why don't you drink some hibiscus tea?"

The Pocketknife

"EVERYTHING HAS ITS TIME," MY mom said once when we had planted violet seeds in a flower pot. "Don't forget to water the pot once a day and wait to see what happens next. You won't believe your eyes when the first sprout appears." Then, she put some seeds into the tiny hole she had made with her finger in the soil and slowly covered it up.

While she watched, I added a few drops of water on top. Afterward, it was my responsibility to take care of it. A couple of weeks later, a weak sprout popped out with slowly unfurling green leaves. It was growing. Once a week, in the early morning, after I had put on my school uniform, I used to go to the window and water it. And one day, while I went to do that, half asleep, I saw a purple bloom. My eyes became wide open, and I quickly called my mom. We stared at the young violet flower with great excitement. On that day, my mom made a cake as a small celebration. I was ten then. Two years later, I found her dead in bed. The next day, the villagers put her into the ground like a violet seed. They covered the top of the grave just as carefully.

"Everything has its time." Her soft voice rang in my ears. The first week after her death, I still had hope. I believed that one day, sooner or later, she would open the front door quietly, go directly to the kitchen, and start to cook without even saying, "Hello, I'm back." My eyes were locked on the closed front door. It didn't move.

Our friends had stopped coming by to say, "We're sorry for your loss."

My dad was as silent as the door. He didn't want to move his lips. He didn't want to talk about her death—the big, black hole in the house. But, one day, she would return, and our home would be the same again, warm and alive. I even prepared myself to be surprised when I saw her in the kitchen. Probably one or two tears would come, and my mouth would be open.

She would stop cooking when our eyes met and clean her muddy hands on her favorite kitchen apron—she never let me wear it—and say, "Oh, I was just a little sick. You didn't need to make such a fuss: a funeral, countless tears, heartbreaking wishes, and lonely silence. Why did you put away all my clothes? Don't you think it was too soon? Finding my apron gave me such a hard time. Why did you put it in the darkest, deepest corner of the basement?" Then she would have paused, glanced at me with her green eyes, and continued chiding, "It was in a dusty bag! Don't you think it was too soon? What's the rush? I didn't dare to start looking for my gardening gloves. God knows where you put my earrings. Now, everyone is hungry and waiting for me to cook something. I haven't even had time to take a shower yet; I've been trying to fix this mess in the kitchen." Her face would have been muddy, and the dress under her apron should have been ragged.

Her bright and shining eyes would have examined me in a second. Then, with a crackle in her voice, she should have continued, "You look thinner. Haven't you been eating anything while I've been gone!" A few seconds later, she might have looked around at the food there, confused like a clumsy thief. "If you put even one spoon of this stuff in your mouth, you'll get sick. Anyway, one bag of fresh *börülce* made me forget the horror. I cleaned it up immediately and put some olive oil in a pan. But where is the garlic?"

I would have begged her to keep talking because I so missed her voice. Her sound should have traveled all through the house, sticking to its white walls, never to leave again. At this point, she should have stopped here in contemplation of something. Instead, she spoke for the last time without taking her eyes off me and whispered, "Take good care of yourself because I won't be here anymore."

Her muddy hands never opened that damn front door, and I gave up waiting in vain. My anger grew when my hope vanished. I wanted to kick the flowerpot because it reminded me of my mother. I imagined her hands still working there. Instead, I should have thrown the violets and watched them shatter to pieces with the soil scattered all over the place and the flowers helpless on the ground. The purple violet would dry up and die without realizing what had happened—the memory of the hands that once carefully potted that soil would be gone forever.

I returned to thinking of that tiny, brown seed and how it transformed into purple leaves years later while walking back home from the Pearl Seller. The aroma of the hibiscus tea was still in my mouth, and my tongue was burnt from drinking it in one gulp in excitement.

When the Pearl Seller had mentioned the wound, the same anger had come back. The wound reminded me of my mom's death and my ridiculous hope that she would return one day. Her death hurt me in a way that would never heal. Would Elmados Elmuhattel's appearance add another one? No way. Instead of smashing them, I had taken good care of the violets. They continued to bloom. I would trim its leaves, put them in new pots, and gift its offspring to others. But I could still destroy the purple flowers in a second. What about my mom's hands? They are still there, growing. For some reason, it comforts me to think of it this way. And a ghost's ominousness wasn't enough to shatter the flowerpot.

Sometimes destroying memories can be liberating. Sometimes it's the right thing to do. It's a rebellion against the passing of time. The more I protested, the louder time ticked away, ignoring my presence. I felt as if I was a twig about to be carried out by the waves. One that would never end up on a distant shore but drowned by a swallowing whirlpool and left to the depths of the sea. However, I restrained myself and did not strike the violet pot. The wise might call it maturity; I was just trying not to mess up.

I was still angry when I jumped back over the marble wall. And whenever I got angry, I would remember the pot and want to obliterate it and, hopefully, the painful memory with it. My thoughts paced back and forth; "Break it!" or "Calm down," torn between my emotions. I should have gotten rid of it long ago, scattering its soil into the sky.

But the Pearl Seller had given me a glimmer of hope with his words, "He will go back."

But when?

It was still summer, and the plums were ready to pick, red and ripened. While there was no plum tree in my garden, the branches of the neighbor's stretched out into it, ignorant of any borders. The masses of red fruit hanging on them seemed larger than the rest of the parts of the tree holding them up. The tree's limbs bowed over as if to complain about the load they were carrying. And every now and then, a plum fell to the ground with a thud, to the point where the ground was decorated with a sort of green with red polka dots design.

Elmados, unaware of what was going on, lay among them, leaning his back against the garden fence. He wore a hat on his head. Where did he find it? It hid his face, most of his black wavy hair, and his ears. He was working on something. He lifted his head up slightly when he saw me coming. The dark light in his eyes startled me. I didn't want him to know what I had done that day. I took a deep breath and, without saying anything, picked up some plums off the ground. I wiped them off on my skirt, went into the house, and threw them into a pan with some water and spices. While I waited for the pan to boil, I went into the living room and sat next to the violets. Their purple blooms looked back at me. They were waiting. I gave it some water and kissed its leaves. I can't break it! I'd break a part of my heart with it. By then, the smell of the cooking plums and cinnamon had started to invade the whole house. I added some honey and turned off the stove. I was feeling better and went back to the garden. My anger had left.

Elmados was still there, whittling a piece of driftwood. The bird's chirping mingled with the songs of cicadas and the sounds of his carving. They were the only things that filled the air between us. At first, I didn't dare speak. But after some time had passed, I coughed, hoping Elmados would turn his dark eyes on me. His hat was like a dark, heavy lid, impossible to lift open. His hands still worked away.

At last, I spoke, "It's so hot today!"

The sound from his carving was the only thing that answered. I moved beside him and tried to peek under the hat. The pocketknife shone in his hands.

While I stared at him, I asked, "What are you making?"

Small shavings had started to coat the grass around Elmados.

The black wall spoke, "I remember."

I was delighted at the response and became excited. I brushed off the leaves stuck to my skirt and asked, "Yes! What did you remember?"

He didn't answer and just continued to whittle away. Then, after a while, he set the pocketknife down at his side and, without looking at me, spoke, "An image has leaked out of my salty memory, albeit in bits and pieces, something that happened before I died. I wonder if it all will come out." The sailor picked the knife back up and continued carving. Elmados blew away the shavings on the piece of wood with his lips and lifted it up to examine it.

There was a thud from behind as another plum fell to the ground again.

The Pearl Seller's warning echoed in my ears, *"He might hurt you."*

I got up and started to walk back into the house. "Well, I'm happy for you. I made some plum compote. Do you want some?"

He just said, "No," and started to whistle a tune. A melody I've never heard before. A melody from the sea.

The Galley

THE MELODY OF THE SEA that Elmados spoke into my ears stayed with me for a while. And yet he became quiet and busied himself with what he was working on as time passed. His hands never seemed to stop as he used his pocketknife to carve away at a piece of driftwood. It was as if he were a possessed sculptor chipping away at a bit of marble with no apparent vision in mind that any ignored onlookers could discern. He was only driven by his own troubled memories. Elmados didn't know what would emerge in the end, and if he had a guess of what it might be, he didn't dare share it. But it was clear that the sailor was struggling with his past, and the bits of it leaking into his mind were tormenting him. Elmados was coming to understand; remembering was a heavy burden. Our past can break us, especially for a soul that rejects the fact that they had died. I could see the pain but didn't want to interrupt him. Then, after a while, he got up and left. And for a couple of weeks, I didn't see him again. I had no idea where he had gone.

As the days passed, the figs hanging from the tree ripened, a sign of summer's end. Their eventual decay was yet another reminder of the cyclical nature of life. As winter approached, the fig tree's branches would become naked. Its large leaves would fall to the ground along with any remaining rotted fruit. As would the sounds of the waves become louder with the increasing wind and winter storms. Only a soft rain would quiet the stormy sea down, turning Aegean into a calm lake again. I picked some fresh figs, carefully arranged the fruits in a seagrass basket, and placed it in a sunny spot so the fruits would dry out for winter. Then, I heard a sound coming from the tree. Its upper branches were moving. I walked back to it again. Was it a squirrel or some wild bird looking for food?

Elmados stuck his head through the leaves, looked at me, and asked, "Did we win?"

I smiled, surprised he hadn't asked me that since he had found the pocketknife and become busy carving. It had seemed that he would never revisit the tree nor ask his eminent question again. Yet here he was, looking more alive than ever.

He was cheerful and kept talking while jumping down from the branches, "Can you imagine what would happen if we won?" Then, he stared back and smiled. "We would split the loot first, even before tending to our wounds. Then, we would celebrate in the middle of a pool of blood, like wild animals, and sing songs of victory as we sailed away back home. Have you ever lost a loved one?"

His last question made me shiver and reminded me of my violets. I was going to say something, but he continued before I could start. Elmados revealed that he had lost most of those he loved in one hard fought, victorious battle. But it hadn't stopped him from celebrating with wild songs in a pool of blood. The joy of winning was intoxicating, numbing him to the losses.

"My sorrow and pain were forgotten for a while, until I came home and visited my dead mates' families, I told the news of their heroic deeds and demise, gave their shares of the winnings to their families, and kept my word.

"I have never forgotten their faces. I lived for them, as well, and avenged my fallen mates. Still, that was not my last battle. Many more followed, and sometimes we lost. Losing only increased my determination to win. However, the last battle was different. Oh, if I could only know that we'd won!" He spat on the ground and started to whistle a tune again.

"Elmados! You can't spit where ever you want. This is my garden, and I have rules! Otherwise, I am sorry, but you'll have to find another tree to live under," I scolded him.

He shrugged and said, "Sorry!" He continued to whistle the melody of the sea and rubbed out the place on the ground where he spat with the toe of his foot. The sailor bent down and looked at the basket of figs, still whistling the same tune I'd never heard before. I couldn't take my eyes off him, trying to understand what he was talking about. He had dragged me into a war I did not know. I lifted the fruit basket off the ground and searched for a better place. After some time, I found a better spot. It was going to stay there for a week.

Nevertheless, my mind was on his battle. I had never seen or heard of it: the idea of defeat, blood, and ambition. It left me feeling uneasy. I've never fought in a war. There was no place for such things in our village. Wars had always been something far away, though I had read and heard much about them. Blood and guns had never seemed this close. But now, I could imagine a sea bloody with dead bodies floating all along the surface. One wouldn't know who was from which side, nor from them who had won. The fog would hide the land, and the smoke and fire of battle would make it hard to breathe. Elmados would be one among the dead in the middle of red waters, his lifeless body eventually sinking to the bottom of Aegean like a powerless stone, surrounded by unfamiliar darkness.

The black moss must have wrapped around the sailor's body and held him for centuries. The ships would have sailed away without noticing his absence. The sharks would have tried to get him. But it's hard to take something from the arms of the moss.

Elmados snapped me out of my contemplative state by moving a little closer to me. For a dead man, his movements were agile. Life was beginning to mix in his blood, albeit slowly.

He grabbed me by my arm and said, "Come with me." His fingertips were cold.

"To where?" In an instant, he dragged me from the battlefield back to reality.

Instead of answering, he practically pulled me along the dirt road and led me onto another path. I was confused. The path was narrow and curved. As we ran, I struggled to keep up with him and avoid the tiny branches of the thick olive trees. My skirt caught on a thorn of one of the bushes, and I heard the tearing sound of fabric, but I didn't stop. The sunlight blinded my eyes, and I was sweating.

We went off the path into some trees and, on the other side, came to an empty field full of chamomiles. I fell to my knees, gasping for air.

"Don't you know how to walk slowly? We were almost flying," I said and had no idea where he was taking me, but I was sure it was important to him. My heartbeat returned to normal after resting for a bit. While getting up, I shook my dress, trying to use it as a fan to cool off. A few pieces of grass fell to the ground. Then I put up my hair up into a bun. Feeling the soft coolness of the wind on my neck made me feel better.

I looked around to see the sailor, but instead, I saw a wooden ship before me. The smell of fresh-cut wood was strong. It looked like it was going to anchor soon. Of course, it would have if it had been moored in a port. I touched the freeboard of the galley ship with my fingertips. Its tiny oars were waiting to move. They were placed into small portholes above the freeboard. I rose up on the tips of my toes and tried to see the rest of the hull, the helm, and the masts. The fabric of the sails was ready to unfold. They were each neatly tied to two tall masts with thin strings. Then I bent down, closed one eye, and tried to look through one of the portholes where the oars were sticking out. It was like traveling to another land. A land I'd never been to before. A land that nobody knew about. I saw Elmados staring at me through the portholes on the other side. He didn't blink his brown eyes. I could feel his heart beating.

I stood up again and said, "Elmados! Where did you find this?"

He stood up, too, trying to fix his hair with his hands, "You can't find something like this. I made it!" He had a childish grin on his face, which made him look younger.

"Here is the thing that leaked out of my salty memory," he said, "I had built just such a model when I was a youth, many years before I went to sea. I think my father was there. We might have done it together because I can still hear his words in my ears. While we were working, he would say, 'Carve the ship in your mind first, not in the wood. Your body and hers should be one. You need to feel her in your soul, and then, sailing on the sea, with nothing but the bright stars above. Don't let her disobey you; don't trust anything but yourself. Then, you will have no reason not to win any battle.'"

I hadn't imagined him building such a large model. I just said, "Wow, this is amazing, Elmados!" and stared at the masterpiece. "You learned it from your father?" Still touching it with my fingers. "I wish I could sail on one. I used to go fishing on my father's rowboat when I was little. It was always fun to watch the dolphins jumping around me. And once I traveled to the island, Azure Glass Isle, to visit my uncle, but they were all short trips in small boats. Nothing like a galley."

"The original ones were a little bit bigger than this one, and believe me, you would be begging to return home after a long journey," Elmados declared. He pulled a string, and the ship's sails dropped and opened. The white canvas added to the grandness of the galley. She just needed a bit of wind to be alive.

The sailor pointed to the unfolded cloth of the sails and said, "We used a different type of fabric for these. However, I sneaked by the fishermen and took some of this while they were sleeping. Those poor guys should be thankful I didn't take everything." He winked, made a hush with a finger to his lips, and whispered, "I'm a little bit jealous. It's a better material than we had, and their boats go faster."

I knew those fishermen and was sure they wouldn't know what was missing. Still, I was delighted. "Perhaps your memory is slowly recovering, Elmados! What else do you remember?"

"Just this image so far," he said, shrugging. But then, his eyes left me and went back to the ship, "the rest is covered with salt and water, as you know," and a shadow appeared upon his face again.

"What are you planning to do with it?" I asked.

He said, "Nothing. She won't ever meet Aegean." He paused a little, "But I'm glad I built her. My dad would be proud of me," Elmados said, sounding like a sorrowful boy.

I touched his shoulder and said, "Don't worry." I was still alive but felt as if I had still lost more than Elmados. Don't ask me why. At that moment, I wanted to join a ship headed for who knows where. I wish I hadn't known this damn ghost. Then, I noticed a big eye carved on the bow.

"It's supposed to protect us from the demons of the sea," he said, "I made it mostly using some black moss. I should have made it from marble, but the eyes aren't worth scrounging for. After having been down on the bottom of the sea for so long, I don't believe in its protection. So, I carved its eye quickly without paying too much attention."

I don't know how long we stayed there, but the sunlight had weakened, and it was getting dark. I didn't want to take my eyes off his ship. The galley looked so otherworldly. Even though its hull had never touched the salty water, the ship looked ancient. It was something from the past, something from an unfamiliar history. I could almost hear the rhythm of its oars rowing. I found myself thrilled when I started to imagine all the places it could go, riding up and down on the waves. My head was spinning, and I was laughing along with the whistling of Elmados. For the first time ever, I felt like I didn't belong in the Mossy Village. It was a bizarre feeling. As the sunset, my feet came back to the ground. And I wasn't even wet.

Instead of going straight home, I walked to the shore. Elmados had wanted to stay with his new ship. It was Friday night when villagers would come out and build a bonfire on the beach. The children sometimes would gather up some driftwood in the morning and stack it there.

When I got to the shore, the fire had already been going for some time. Sevim and some old friends of hers were sitting on a bench staring into it, talking in low voices. The old men of the village were sitting closer to the sea. Their voices were louder than the women's. And the children were everywhere, running around waving sticks in the air whose tips had been lit on fire. Some were screaming, and some were laughing. The fire had just started to settle down, and I could smell some corn and potatoes grilling along its edge. When the others saw me, they became quiet, staring at me with sulky faces. Their mouths seemed sealed.

I asked, "What happened?"

The men ignored me.

Sevim said, "We have been discussing the ghost haunting our dreams. Which battle has he been talking about? Why did he come to our village? Questions are waiting to be answered." Her eyes shone in the dark with curiosity. And yet, at the same time, they looked sad and helpless. I couldn't tell them about the galley and what I had talked about with Elmados.

One of the men listening called out, "Is he in your dreams too? You never mentioned it."

A child's scream prevented me from answering. One of the children playing with a flaming stick had burned her arm. Her mom went over and hugged the child.

Sevim handed me her house key and said, "Run! You will find a chest on the right side of the living room. Bring me the yellow bottle in it with some cotton. Hurry!"

As quick as I could, I did what she asked and returned with the articles.

Sevim dribbled out some oil from the yellow bottle onto the cotton and claimed, "St. John's-wort soothes burns instantly."

The girl calmed down but forgot to wipe the tears from her eyes.

Someone shouted, "No more playing with fire! Throw those sticks into the sea right now!"

Everyone had forgotten the ghost. Instead, they started sharing memories about how they had burned themselves while cooking, or making a small fire, or even getting sunburned. But, of course, everyone had a different opinion as to what healed burns best.

I was lucky. I hadn't needed to answer any questions. So, I silently listened as the talking resumed and managed to ask Sevim for some St. John's-wort for myself. Unfortunately, I was not a careful cook.

One Thousand, One Hundred and Seventeen Leaves

THE FOLLOWING DAY, I WOKE up to an unnerving silence. No soft sound of crashing waves nor anything else peaceful or relaxing. I didn't need to look to know that Aegean was an unsettling calm that morning. Over the years, I'd learned how to listen. My ears were attuned to her every sound. And this silence was deafening. Aegean was only a short distance away, but I couldn't bear to face her. It was as if she was ignoring me, choosing instead to keep her secrets hidden beneath a flat, featureless surface. Her wind seemed to have abandoned me, carrying its melodies to other lands. Was I being too sensitive?

I wish someone would comfort me by saying, "Everything will be ok." At least, I wished I could listen to the sweet songs Aegean whistled. But instead, there was only silence. If she didn't feel like singing, that was her choice. I closed the curtains, feeling like a sleepless owl in my dim, cool nest at sunrise, not wanting to be bothered by anyone or anything. My hair was a mess, and my eyes were swollen and red. My weary face looked gloomy in the mirror. If anybody were to touch me, I might explode.

But what about the dried figs in the basket? I had to bring them in from the garden. Otherwise, they would rot in the heat. I needed to put them in a cold, dim place to rest until winter. The seagrass basket was waiting for me next to the fence. I opened the door just a crack, sneaked out and grabbed it quickly, and then retreated back inside. What was I running away from? Perhaps the new galley and the villager's questions were too much to handle, and I needed more time to think. And what about the sea's silence?

When closing the curtains, I spotted some children under an olive tree between the dirt road on one side and the empty field on the other. The tree didn't have an owner; it belonged to the village. We would share the olives when they were ready to harvest. A few paces from the olive tree, the shore started. The tree was across from my window. Two little girls were trying to reach for its branches. However, it was months before harvest time. Why were they picking at the olive buds, then? I opened the curtains a little bit more and stared at them. They were carrying small bags. Did it have something to do with Elmados and his galley? Once back in the house, I stowed the dried fruit basket in the cool of the cellar. With the task done, I made my way to the washroom. I splashed water on my face, trying to scrub away the weariness.

Afterward, I brushed my tangled hair until it was smooth and neat and then changed out of my rumpled clothes into something more appropriate. I looked back into the mirror, "Go outside and learn what is happening. I hope it is not about the damn ghost." Then, I went out. My curiosity led me to walk under the olive tree. Slowly, I walked near to the kids. Their bags were full of olive leaves.

"Why did you pick them?" I asked,

"My mom told me to," one girl said while trying to pull her hair away from her face.

I knew her mother, Zeynep. We tried to be friends when we were young, but somehow, our playing together always ended in fights. One time, I hid where she couldn't find me for hours. When she caught me under that empty box, she was so furious that she threw a rock and hit my forehead. It was swollen and bleeding for a couple of days. Another time, I threw a handful of sand right into her face. It got into her eyes and scratched them. It was painful for her to open them for days. I could hear her crying at night, and she's had a fear of becoming blind ever since. We drifted apart after she got married. Anyway, we were never very close, just two neighbors who didn't prefer talking a lot with each other.

The other girl said, "We have exactly one thousand one hundred and seventeen leaves."

"What will she do with them?"

They both shrugged and without saying anything else, they held up their empty palms to convince me they didn't know and ran back to their house. I followed them out of spite, forgetting my earlier reluctance. It wasn't hard to find Zeynep's among the eighteen similar dwellings. Eighteen stone houses, each with its own name and unique character, sat amidst the olive and fig trees. To an outsider, phrases like "the house with broken tile," "the pomegranate," or "the house at the end" might seem cryptic, but each word held a story understood only by us. Despite every garden containing a fig or a pomegranate tree, only one was called "the fig" or "the pomegranate." For instance, one day, some tiles on my roof broke and fell off. Although I had it repaired over a year later, the house's name remained "the one with the broken tiles."

We named Zeynep's house "The Vineyard" to honor the saplings her husband once brought back from the Black Sea and planted in their yard. In autumn, the garden held an enchanting aroma.

From a distance, I looked towards "The Vineyard." A couple of women were also entering Zeynep's door. It was impossible to recognize who they were. I could only see their backs, and they were wearing headscarves. I didn't want to go there without an invitation. However, I desperately wanted to learn what they planned to do with the leaves. From behind a bunch of bushes, I was able to observe the inside of the house. It was easy to peer inside through their large glass patio doors. The women gathered in the living room, and Sevim was among them.

There was also an unfamiliar face. The strange woman held a stick, and golden rings shone on her fingers. Her gray hair peeked out from under her headscarf, and her green eyes were as bright as the grass. She had to be from another village or town nearby. Zeynep laid a tiny tablecloth on the ground, and the girls emptied bags of leaves onto it. In a hushed silence, the women picked up the leaves, murmuring under their breaths as they blew on each one. Nobody talked with each other. They looked like they were praying for something.

I went past the wooden front door and entered Zeynep's garden. There was one row of grapevines on my left. They became a plant wall with the grapes' leaves tangled in carnation flowers. A dull turtle was moving slowly on the grass. I watched from the doorway as Sevim gestured for me to join them. Stepping over the threshold, I sat beside her, the room's stillness unbroken except for the rustle of leaves.

Zeynep seemed surprised to see me in her house after many years and had forgotten our childish fights. She smiled slightly. I visited her when she was newly married and two years later to congratulate her on her first baby. This was eight years ago, and she never came to see me. Maybe she didn't have any reason to come. Entering her home without any invitation made me nervous. While sitting next to Sevim, I didn't touch any leaves nor talk with any women. I was counting every minute, and time was moving very slowly.

The mound of leaves at the center of the tablecloth steadily dwindled until, eventually, not a single one was left.

I whispered to Sevim, "Who is she?"

"Everyone calls her the Beldam. She is from Mount Ida and just came here to teach us the ritual. Zeynep's husband begged her to come, and finally, the Beldam had mercy. She will return to her shack in a couple of hours," said Sevim.

"Are you making a special *dua*?"

Sevim nodded and whispered back, "Yes, it's for the exorcism of the evil spirit."

I was confused, "Which evil spirit?"

"For the ghost in our dreams."

While looking at the Beldam, I asked, "Does the ghost have an evil soul?" my voice trembled.

"What else could he be?" the Beldam said, and called the children and gave the bags to them, "Throw the leaves to the sea."

"May Allah accept our *duas*," said Zeynep, and everybody said, "Amen," except me.

The suspicious gazes were putting unbearable pressure on me.

"But," I said, "why do you need one thousand a hundred and seventeen leaves?"

"You need to pray in the morning, before noon, and repeat, 'La havle vela kuvvete illa billah' one thousand, one hundred and seventeen times with exactly the same number of olive leaves, and throw the leaves into flowing water. If you don't follow the rules or do it properly, don't wait for your prayers to be answered," the Beldam said. Her green eyes were ice-cold, dull and heartless.

"I've never heard a dua like that before!"

"It's an old one; very few people know this," said the Beldam, "Otherwise, I wouldn't be here." Her eyes were like shards of ice, merciless and brutal, and I was averse to their piercing stare.

I instinctively wanted to protect Elmados and said, "But just a single question doesn't make him evil. He's been asking if his side won the battle or not."

"If he was a good spirit, he would know the answer before he died," said the wicked woman with her freezing eyes.

While Zeynep was handing the tea, the other women kept talking and questioning me, "You never say something about the ghost. You didn't even tell us whether you ever saw him in your dreams."

The women stirred their tea with sugar and took the first sip of it.

Zeynep brought everyone some *poğaça* and *sarma*.

I heard the jingle of the ceramics.

"What could I have seen differently from you? I don't know anything other than what you know," I said with frustration.

I got up quickly, not making eye contact with any of them, and left Zeynep's house without saying, "Goodbye."

I WASN'T THINKING PROPERLY WHILE running to the shore, and I couldn't stop my tears. Anger, sadness, fear, hate, and love were blundering inside me. I passed the dull turtle, the small grapevine, the wooden door of the garden, the dirt road, and left behind the houses in my back. The two girls were preparing to throw the leaves into the water on the pier. They were as calm as the sea. I ignored them, ran to the dock, and suddenly jumped into the water with my regular clothes. One thousand one hundred and seventeen green leaves fell to the sea like rain after me, and my tears mixed with salty water. Once submerged, I felt like a heavy stone sinking slowly under the sea without any effort. I wept under the sea, and my breaths made thousands of bubbles. Maybe one thousand one hundred and seventeen bubbles were not enough to stop the villagers. As my crying slowed and my heartache ebbed, the sea seemed to understand my turmoil.

In response, the coldness of Aegean wrapped around me like a mother's arms. It was an unexpected comfort, pulling me away from the pain and sorrow that had driven me into its depths. My crying gently subsided, and I swam without looking at the leaves or the kids. I paddled to an inlet nobody knew and sat at the edge of the shore with my wet clothes, then swam again. It took all my day. When I returned to the pier, it was already dark. On the way home, my feet were leaving wet marks behind me. I was shaking and felt powerless. While changing my clothes, I heard a knock on my window. It was Elmados.

He said, "Where the hell have you been? I couldn't find you all day."

Without answering him, I closed the curtains and went to sleep. The last thing I saw were Elmados' dark and worried eyes.

The Sunset's Color

IT WAS STILL NIGHT WHEN I woke for what must have been the umpteenth time, as though the sun had pledged never to rise again. The shards of green ice beside the windowsill were melting, and the drops falling from them were tapping out an unbearable rhythm. I imagined the Beldam getting closer with every drop, her whispers,

"He is evil," curling around me like smoke. Paralyzed on my bed, I wanted to scream, but my voice refused. I glanced around yet again, my eyes searching for her. The room still lay drowned in darkness, devoid of any other presence. Fear held me captive, stymieing any urge to move. As much as I wanted to believe it was merely a recurring nightmare, I needed to make sure the wicked woman was truly absent. Again, I closed my eyes, yielding once more to the clutches of sleep, and found myself in a forest. A lone hut loomed in the distance. The Beldam was there, holding her long stick with her fingers full of gold rings. There was an odd sound whenever the woman struck the ground with her staff.

I opened my eyes again. This time, I was able to will myself to rise and went to the kitchen to get a drink. I was cold and sweaty. I put on a sweater over my pajamas, opened the door, breathed in the cool air, and sat in the garden for a while, watching the stars. The darkness of the night was a safer place than my dreams. Even though I wasn't very keen to do so, I went back inside, took off my sweaty flannel, and returned to sleep. The Beldam continued to haunt me. Every creak of the bed seemed to echo with her whispers, turning once comforting blankets into a battlefield. Her piercing eyes didn't promise anything good. My nightmares continued night after night. I don't know how many sunrises I missed while lost in their labyrinths.

"He can wound you easily," said the Pearl Seller; however, he never suggested that Elmados was evil. I trusted the wise man much more than the wicked woman. How did Zeynep's husband find her?

Nights were like a bright stage with stars, and the moon changed from full to crescent and occasionally disappeared entirely, swallowed by the velvet black. Sometimes, the fog cloaked the land, rendering the stars invisible. Yet, I found a strange comfort in watching this gloom-laden stage unfold. The Beldam was still tormenting me. Many days passed.

One morning, I awoke with sunlight dazzling in my eyes. The window beside my bed was open, with the curtains fluttering in the wind. I could see the blue sky and felt a weight had been lifted from me. That night, the whispers of the Beldam had left. My body was still in pain, and I had a slight headache. However, I was sure that my old self was back. I lifted myself up to shake the sleep off and was shocked to find Elmados sitting at the foot of my bed, his face pale with anxiety. Struggling, I opened my mouth to speak, but words didn't come out. Again, I was powerless.

Elmados saw me struggling and the perplexed look on my face. He stirred some concoction in a copper plate with a spoon and spoke, "Spare your questions. Breaking in was as easy as taking candy from a child. Did you think I would abandon you to languish in illness?" His voice was full of concern. "If you had seen yourself the night you threw the curtains shut on me—your lips were the color of purple, your eyes bloodshot. I've been quietly keeping an eye on you. For days, you've shut out the world. I was even a little afraid you might die. Then, one night, you appeared like an apparition, opening the front door just to stare at the stars. You sat there for hours, not moving an inch." His words hung in the air for a moment before he continued, "You reminded me of a shadow from my past and a treatment I had invented for healing her." He held up the copper plate for me to see, revealing a paste the color of sunset. He scooped up a spoonful of it and put it in my mouth. It had a bitter taste, but I forced it down.

"The Beldam thinks you are evil, Elmados," I wanted to tell him but couldn't speak, "The villagers wish you would leave." The words were boulders lodged in my throat, finding their escape only through the tears that cascaded down my cheeks.

He moved a little closer, enveloped me in a hug, and said, "Don't worry, you'll be fine. This remedy is so powerful it might even be able to bring the dead back to life. Get some sleep." His warm breath on my neck was like a healing potion for my weak body. No, he can't be evil.

The recovery was a long and grueling process. I cloaked myself in a woolen blanket, which served as my sanctuary from the outside world. I yearned for peace, a resolution between the ghost and the villagers. Yet, showing them Elmados' galley might only incite their wrath by giving them something they could direct their anger at. They might burn it down or rip it to pieces, not desiring to understand. As if it wasn't enough, those villagers would never forgive me. Despite the looming danger, there was a strange force tethering me to him, an inexplicable feeling. But if Elmados remained, I knew the Beldam would stop at nothing to drive him away.

Elmados sat next to me whenever I awoke, and each time, he put another spoon of the sunset-colored paste in my mouth. We didn't talk much, but his presence and his herbal mixture made me feel better.

During one of those periods, while I was awake, I was able to converse again without difficulty and said, "I've thought of a name for your weird concoction."

"What is it?" asked Elmados.

"Sunset's Color."

"Hmm... I never thought of it that way, but it sounds good. Actually, I called it Hawthorn Paste. However, comparing it with yours, mine sounds too plain and simple. The Sunset's Color is more poetic and carries with it some melancholy."

"It had a bitter taste, but after days of having nothing else in my mouth, it started to taste better."

"I'm glad to hear that," Elmados smiled, "Finding hawthorn was not easy this time of year. For a sick person, it is more valuable than gold for its healing properties."

"Who was the shadow?"

Elmados was startled and opened his dark eyes widely, "Which shadow?"

"The one you said you healed with this paste."

"You don't forget anything,"

"Because I'm not dead. Also, a kind heart healed me fast. Yes, you were telling me who they were."

"Was I?" Elmados asked as he got up from the foot of my bed and lingered for a while. Then, as he stood by the open window, he explained, "I don't remember very well. Maybe she was my sister, maybe not. The shadow that was a person has trickled out of my salty memory. Some snippets are left: A sick woman in her bed and this medicine are all that I remember. I sometimes wonder if she ever got better and how did she eventually die."

"It's strange that you remember your remedy and yet forgot who she was."

"I think you've recovered," he said, "You don't need me here anymore. Allow me to leave you for a while, but don't forget to take more of the Sunset's Color. Finish all the paste. Why don't you get out some? Go for a walk. Eat something special. Meditate and take deep breaths. Swim if you want. And get better as soon as possible. I'll be away for a while." He took some hawthorns and his knife from his ragged pockets and put them onto the chest. "Peel and boil the fruit well. Crush it, add one tablespoon of apple vinegar, and if you wish, a teaspoon of honey. The real challenge, however, involves collecting water from five different fountains during the night and adding five drops from each to the boiling hawthorn-infused water." Then he left the room. The pocketknife's blade glimmered in the light.

Before I could forget it, I got up and wrote his recipe down on paper: "Elmados' Sunset's Color," with the fruits, formula, and the knife resting on the door chest.

The next afternoon, there was a knock on my door three times in a hurry. Elmados wouldn't knock; it wasn't his habit. It was Zeynep. Without taking off her beige cardigan, she sat on the sofa as if planning to leave immediately.

I made some tea for her. After the first sip, she started to talk, "Actually, I came to visit you a few days ago, but nobody was here. Did you go somewhere?" She fixed her curious eyes on me and kept talking, "You didn't look well the day the Beldam came. Hopefully, the ghost will leave us soon. And we will all breathe easier then. It will be soon. I feel it."

"I was ill, but now I'm much better. Thanks for asking," I said and listened to Zeynep's boring speech with patience. I recognized why I hadn't spoken to her in years.

While she was leaving, she invited me to another meeting, "But," she said, "this one, it will be at night, and we will gather around the fire. We are now waiting for the waves and the wind to subside. I'll send my daughter to you with the particulars."

I had no intention of participating in a ritual to expel Elmados. If he chose to leave, it would have been of his own volition.

Forgotten

THE SEA DID NOT CALM down for a long time. It was as if Aegean did not want the villagers to gather and pray for Elmados' expulsion. All their hopes were dashed. Elmados knew nothing. After my recovery, he disappeared for a while. I had no idea where he went. A few days after Zeynep's visit, he reappeared under the fig tree. I had just made myself breakfast but hadn't yet taken the first bite when my eyes looked up from the meal and met his sunken gaze.

He asked, "Did we win?" and seemed to have forgotten that he had helped me recover and all about the concoction he had prepared. I was rather perplexed.

"Do you want to live, or do you want to find out whether or not you won?" I asked, a bit annoying.

The sailor lowered his head and started to fumble through his ragged clothes with his hands, "Both!" He acted like a reckless pupil who never tires of getting it wrong.

"You can choose only one."

"Let me think," he responded.

"You have been thinking, for all I know, for a thousand years, and you haven't decided yet!"

He shouted back, "When you are a spirit, you have lots of time to think!" There was something broken and crumbling in his voice. I may have been too hard on him.

"May the waves wash you away before you decide," I said, unable to contain my rage, "or we'll wait another thousand years!"

There was a deep silence. Elmados was motionless. "I want to live," he said after a brief pause. Realizing I didn't believe him, he repeated, "I want to live. But how?" Questions gathered in his dead eyes.

Indeed, what was necessary for Elmados to live? His question opened a small gap in my soul. I didn't know how to fill it, a void that grew larger by the minute, a void that swallowed me more and more, a void that was hard to cope with.

Elmados looked at me innocently, waiting patiently for an answer to his question. What made him think I would find an answer? I turned my head away, afraid he would see I had no answer. I stood up, paced the garden as if I had forgotten something, and circled back. He followed but remained silent. I bent down and examined the tomatoes I had planted last month. There was nothing to look at, really. They were all unripe.

I could no longer stand his innocent gaze, so I blurted out the first thing that came to my mind: "Let's find you some new clothes first."

He looked at me as if seeing me for the first time. "What's wrong with my clothes?" he asked. "Is that the only problem?"

I got up from where I was crouching and touched his sun-bleached clothes more determinedly, "You need to look like a human again and so that others won't be scared of you. If we fix you up, if you look no different from any other passerby, no one will care whether you are alive or dead. If you cut your hair and shave, it will help a lot."

He was skeptical, unable to believe he could come back to life.

"Just try it. You have nothing to lose," I said.

He became serious. A sadness he couldn't suppress crept into his voice, "I have a lot to lose!"

Finding clothes for Elmados was easier than I thought. He was a little taller and more built than most of the people of the Mossy Village, but his body was not out of the norm. There was an old chest in the village that was rarely opened. It contained clothes like pants and shirts, put there so that those in need could take them, clothes that had been cleaned and mended so that they were like new. This chest was at the foot of the marble wall that bordered the village. After some hesitation, I took out from it a plain white shirt and a pair of brown pants. A nice wool scarf and some gloves at the bottom caught my eye.

"Try these on," I said, handing them to Elmados.

After he had changed into them, and shaved, he looked quite handsome. The clothes, gathering dust in the trunk, looked very different on him. The ghostly quality of his body had left or been covered up. His wavey hair straightened down onto his forehead. He wasn't sure where to put his hands for a while. Elmados seemed excited and fragile. A slight regret flowed through my heart. But the decision was made. He would no longer haunt my figs, nor would he ask me every day, "Did we win?" Most importantly, he would never visit the village again. I had helped him decide, and now had no choice but to help him.

He began to ask other questions, "Where will I go? What will I do?" He was as excited as a child, wanting to explore the world.

"Don't go too far away," I said, "Let's think and make a plan." I drew a map of the Mossy Village and Aegean for him. "This is the east, and this is the west side of it. The marble wall is southwest of the village, and the empty field is towards the northeast." Even though it was unnecessary, I drew the black moss, fig, and olive trees. I didn't want him to forget my house so that he could return anytime and find it instantly.

"Walking to the town of Kamasis takes a couple of hours, but you can find more opportunities there," I stated, adding it to the map.

"Let's go tomorrow," he said as he glanced at the map, folded it, and put it in his pocket.

I wanted to ask, "It's a bit early, isn't it?" but I gave in and instead said, "Great!"

The following day, Elmados was ready to go. We walked silently along the road without talking to each other until we reached the town's docks. Kamasis was busy and crowded. There was a market in the main square where fish, seafood, fruit, and vegetables were sold. The smell of hot bread from a nearby bakery was in the air.

"Buy goods from the sunken ship!" some market vendors shouted out into the air.

A distracted customer bumped into my shoulder. A boy carrying milk jugs on his shoulders, splashing milk, headed for the bazaar. A horse neighed behind me. Both Elmados and I were stunned, unaccustomed to the noise of the city.

"Are you sure?" Elmados asked. "Is it really easier to live here? You said it was open to opportunities?"

"What do you take me for, a scholar or a dervish? I've lived nowhere but the Mossy Village all my life. I'm not here to give you life lessons. You will find your own path, Elmados."

He nodded, convinced yet uneasy and thoughtful. I felt no different from him.

We sat on the first bench we found by the sea, comforted by the familiar waves. The blue sky was clear, and the wind was still. Was this the calm before the storm? Or was it the sadness of the impending farewell descending upon us? Two men started a fight behind us. A boy passing by stared at us while gnawing on a piece of a dry baguette. Its crumbs stuck to his cheeks.

A beggar with a hunchback asked for money. "Please," he said, opening his palm. When he saw no desire from us, he shouted in rage "Go to hell!"

A Romani woman holding a bunch of red roses in one hand came by and asked, "Shall I tell you your fortune?" While patiently waiting for our reply, she walked around us and observed. She wore a golden necklace, and old blue veins could be seen through her thin, translucent skin. One of the buttons on her brown shirt was missing. When she couldn't get an answer out of us, she gave up and left us alone. We were like two statues, but time was passing.

Shortly, I said, "Go find a boat and crew to join, but not a warship, of course! Maybe a fishing boat. I'm sure they need a talented sailor who knows the sea well far from shore."

He said, "Take care of my galley." After a short hesitation he continued, "I'm tired of eating figs every day. It's hard to live in other's nightmares. And nobody's ever invited me to their dinner table."

I said, "Don't make me cry!" and turned my back to him. There was an emptiness under the fig tree. For a while, I couldn't climb the tree's branches nor eat his fruit. He reminded me of someone who had been hungry for many years. It was the last time I saw Elmados. He never came back to the village again.

THE WAVES FORGOT ME. THEY enveloped my feet without bringing me anything. I could hear the sound of her withdrawing. Every morning when I woke up, I saw that Aegean had gone a little further out than the day before. The urchins' wet, brown needles moved in a hurried panic to catch up to it. They had lost their home and didn't know what else to do except follow the water. Minute by minute, they were drying up. The brilliant pebbles along the old shoreline, with no water to coat them, had lost their luster. A thin white film of salt left by the sea covered the dried black moss and changed its color to a whitish-brown pastel. They looked like an old witch's long, messy hair. A crab had left its stone and started to crawl confused along the beach, but it didn't know where to go.

Since Elmados' departure, the villagers' dreams had become peaceful again, but looking out to sea, they sensed something strange.

Fatima said, "It's just the tide! The waves will return."

Sevim said, "I've never seen a tide stay out like that before in my life!"

Somebody shouted from the window, "Others have destroyed our world!"

I was silent and felt guilty, thinking that Aegean was angry with me. Perhaps, this time, I had hurt her unintentionally. Maybe I should make some fig jam. I gathered up the tiny ones and knocked on Sevim's door.

I said, "Can you teach me how to make fig jam?"

She nodded without saying anything. I cooked thirty jars of jam that day and gave them out to everyone in the Mossy Village.

CHAPTER THREE

The Sleeping Simurgh and The Witch

IT TOOK AZRA A WHILE to come to terms with the gaping void that Elmados had left behind. The inky darkness beneath the fig tree seemed to breathe on its own; it shrank and expanded erratically, threatening to engulf her whole. There were moments when Azra felt that she was living inside that hollow emptiness as if it was all that existed in the world. However, as time passed, it receded into an insignificant black spot, barely noticeable.

Meanwhile, the waves of Aegean continued to withdraw. Ominous whispers of change fluttered through the Mossy Village. Azra held a faint spark of hope that one day, the waves would return. This hope was fragile, ready to be snuffed out at any moment.

The small clearing where the villagers had once swum in the water was now parched sand. Its sea plants had withered and crumbled under the sun's rays. They were joined with the skeletal remains of unfortunate fish and empty seashells. Yet the sea's salt still lingered in the air.

The people of the Mossy Village were in the early days of their catastrophe. The fishermen's boats became stuck in the sand, their nets empty. The gleam in people's eyes faded, and their faces turned grim. The curse seemed to be growing, touching something new every day. Then the fishermen left the village, searching for places Aegean had not yet abandoned. Having lost hope, everyone was filled with the thought of exile. No one knew how to live without the waves and what they brought. Azra, the young woman of the village, said farewell to her dear friend Fatima. Fatima, who left the Mossy Village in a carriage with everything they could carry with them. One by one, the lights in the houses went out. Yet, Azra chose to stay.

When the Birds Left the Earth

ALL ROADS IN THE MOSSY Village lead to only one place: the sea. The people here are quiet. Its inhabitants have learned the silent language of Aegean waves from a tender age. However, the few people who chose to stay didn't know how to live alone on an abandoned shore after the disaster, and Sevim had grown weary of the silence. One late afternoon, she sat along the pebbled former coast, lost in the vastness, while envisioning the absent blue waves. An invisible dog in the forest barked for a long time, and then others around joined in, forming a choir. None of them had an owner. No, she didn't know how to live in another land. Her whole world was here, and nothing existed for her beyond its borders.

From afar, Azra noticed Sevim's unusual silence. Usually, by this time, the old lady would have passed by the house, bombarding Azra with long-winded questions, speeches, and complaints. "I shouldn't have left her alone," Azra mused. "Ever since I learned to make fig jam from her, she's kept her distance." Without saying even hi, Azra went over and sat next to the oldest lady in the village.

Sevim had some small white pebbles she had collected from the old shore resting on the top of her skirt. She took a deep, shaky breath as if summoning memories from a time long ago without moving her gray, pale eyes. They continued to stare at the gap left by the sea, "You always asked me why I don't go near the sea and swim. Do you think I don't love Aegean?" She spoke very slowly, as if in a dream, "In the past, I wasn't as resentful or talkative. I would accept what the sea brought with resignation, and like everyone else, I would respond to the waters with silence. I was a cheerful child who liked to play in the sea. Do you know why I haven't left the village yet? Because I am sure that Aegean will return. Things vanish and then reappear. You'll see. The black moss taught me that. If you care to listen..."

Then, she turned her gaze towards Azra.

"I have a hope that the sea will return too. But it's now a faint hope. It fades more every day that passes. But please go on. Of course, I would like to hear what you have to say," Azra replied.

Sevim turned her gaze back to the void and continued. She spoke as if she was talking to herself. "Today, as I was staring at the void left by the waters, I saw a dead seagull. It had the glimmer of an unfinished journey left in its dead eyes. Its neck was broken, and its beak was left open by death. A few feathers from its wings lost in its last struggle surrounded it. They reminded me of a time when all the birds had vanished from the world. As a young girl, I thought troubles and calamities affected only others. Years ago, before you were born, Azra, the birds left the skies. Their sudden, horrible deaths were like a slap in the face as their bloody bodies fell to the ground. The sky was full of thousands upon thousands of their lost feathers floating in the air. They fell, covering every window sill and doorstep. The shore was littered with bird skeletons. Everyone had their own interpretation: It might be a bird plague. A poisonous seed that the birds love to eat. Perhaps the sea brought some illness to them. Maybe Allah sent it to test us. Or perhaps it was just a temporary nightmare. Regardless of the cause, we were clueless as to how to make the birds return.

"Until one day, hidden between the rocks, I found a strange feather. And then, another one, and another. I collected them in my hands. Some of their tips were stained with blood. Their complementary hues suggested that they came from the same source. Entranced, I followed their trail, picking up each of the feathers, expecting to find a carcass at its end. Where it led, the waves became still, with feathers floating softly on the water's surface. I was soon knee-deep in water, surrounded by the black moss. I was so engrossed that I hadn't noticed the water gradually rising from my ankles to my knees. A slight shiver went down my spine when my feet touched the plant, but I was too busy chasing the feathers to be that bothered by it. I wasn't afraid of a bit of seaweed wrapped around my bare feet. I kept moving forward. I tried swimming around them. The plant resembled a dark underwater forest, eventually becoming unavoidable. The water became deep, but the tangled web grew so thick they buoyed me up."

"I used to be scared of the black moss when I was little," said Azra.

"Fears protect us. But, sometimes it's pointless fighting with it," Sevim claimed and kept talking, "Of course, I was young then, fast and agile. Now, I would panic and drown in a spoonful of water, but I didn't have such worries then. I followed the feathers the bird left and kept collecting them. There was no end to their trail in sight.

"A thorn's sting in my heel startled me, causing me to lose balance and plunge into the sea. The moss started to wrap around my body. At that moment, I wanted to go back to land. I struggled to stay up, but keeping my head above water was becoming harder and harder. The plant was dragging me further out to sea and trying to pull me down towards its roots. I gripped the feathers in my hand tightly and opened my eyes. The light underwater was getting faint. I couldn't breathe.

"At that time, in the Mossy Village, there lived a woman named Elif Nana. She was one of my mother's close friends. May her soul rest in peace. She passed away like many others. As the black moss ensnared me, memories of Elif Nana's warnings echoed: 'Beware of the dark tendrils' magic.' Elif Nana would open her eyes wide and whisper, 'Don't let them take you in,' they would make me shiver.

Once, I told my mother, 'Don't listen to that crazy Elif,' she interrupted me and said, 'Her mind goes and comes back. She should be ashamed of herself.'

"As the dark algae dragged me into the sea's depths, memories of Elif Nana flashed before me. 'Be careful,' she repeated a thousand times in my memory, 'black moss is not safe.'

"Darkness enveloped me. For a moment, all was void and disorienting, like a dreamscape shifting from one scene to another without warning. The familiar salty coldness of Aegean was replaced by a colder, biting sensation that prickled my skin."

Azra got up excitedly, no longer able to contain herself; she interrupted Sevim, "Colder than Aegean?! It must have been scary," and she flinched as if shivering from the cold.

Sevim sighed, her gaze distant, and continued, "Exactly! I was perplexed. My body had become used to the temperature of the sea, but it was getting colder and colder. My skin felt as if it was burning because of the icy water. However, a surprising view met my eyes just as death seemed imminent. Rising out of the water and through a thin layer of ice, I found myself in a mountain lake amid snow in a foreign land with a mountain's peak nearby."

"It never snows on Mount Ida!" said Azra.

"It was much higher than Mount Ida," said Sevim, raising her hands to the sky. It was as if she had stepped into that snowy land again. "She turned around and gestured towards Mount Ida in the distance. Nevertheless, the moss that brought me there was covered with tiny ice crystals. When I grabbed ahold of the moss with my other hand as if for help, the crystals broke off and scattered. The thin layer of ice covered the lake's surface, but in some places, it had small openings, and the ice around it had cracked like glass. I tried walking on it. The surface was slippery but passable as long as it didn't break. I approached one of the openings and bent over to look. It was dark. Full of secrets. The moss at the water's surface and underneath the ice made the area around it black.

"I crossed the lake and started walking into the unknown towards the mountain. Everything was covered in snow, my feet sinking in and out of it. Yet, the cold barely touched them. The mountain's peak stood next to me like a silent giant. I couldn't see a smoking chimney, a small hut, or any other sign of life. I wheeled around and tried to make my way back to the lake. The snow did not make it easygoing. It didn't matter; I wanted to get out of here.

"Just then, I stumbled upon a bulging form from beneath the snow. I got up and looked at the lake full of black moss behind me. Running away would be pointless. Slowly, I dug and started clearing the snow away from the object. I didn't want to draw attention to myself. I was dazzled by the colorful feathers that appeared, and it seemed so warm. The creature lying underneath the snow was a giant bird. The bird must have felt uncomfortable where it was lying because it moved a little. After some moments, it moved, and the snow covering it fell off, making it easier for me to see the bird. Afraid it might harm me, I moved back but continued staring at it intensely."

Breaking away from the grip of the past, Sevim played with the small stones on her lap, "Aegean will return; that was what I wanted to say. I'm starting to feel tired. I need a break," said Sevim. And she stood up, trying not to let any of the pebbles fall to the ground. But a few pebbles rolled onto the ground. There were beads of sweat on her forehead. Her dry, wrinkled lips kept moving as she murmured to herself. She started to walk away, ignoring Azra. The old lady staggered and looked like she could use a staff.

Azra had listened carefully and was shocked by what she had heard, but when Sevim started to leave, ignoring her, she was hurt. "Nothing that comes from this dark stuff ever gives us any happiness!" she cried, "Why is everything it sends foul?" And she started to run to catch up to Sevim.

The dry lips of the old lady were still murmuring.

Azra was breathless from catching up, "You are in good condition for your age. It's unbelievable that you can walk this fast without a stick. I wish the story you told me wasn't true, but..." She stopped walking, picked some dry moss from the ground, and said, "I'm exhausted with this dark trouble. It abducts us to strange lands and brings us lost spirits. Elmados' lies were painful enough. Damn the day I found him in the moss. Now, you're talking about a bird living in a land of snow. Or are you going to say you've gone to Mount Qaf? I wish the sea would have taken me with her. Aegean was my only friend." Azra's exclamations echoed through the emptiness of the inlet, "Why won't you talk to me?" She started to walk again.

Sevim was walking hunched over with her hands clasped behind her back, not responding to Azra. After trying to calm down by taking some deep breaths, Azra found herself still upset. "Won't you tell me the rest of it?"

Again, the old lady didn't answer. They came in front of Sevim's house. She opened the wooden door, turned to Azra, and said, "You will learn. Wait for me here."

Azra worriedly paced back and forth near the entrance, grumbling, "Nothing is the same, even Sevim."

The wooden door squeaked open, and Sevim's head appeared from behind it, "Don't worry, and when you are ready, start reading. She handed the young woman what looked like an ancient journal, "I just don't have the energy to talk more. Going back through those past memories has made me weak. I want to be alone for a while. Good thing I scribbled something down when I returned to Mossy. You can read the rest of it from that. Good night." And the wooden door closed.

Azra took the journal and went home without saying another thing. The daylight was fading. She lit some candles in the room and tried to push her annoyance aside. Before she opened the book, she again took a deep breath and tried to manage her thoughts. She knew that the black moss was magical, but she didn't know what it was capable of. She had known many stories about the village before but had never heard about a time when all the birds had disappeared. As she opened Sevim's notes, she was taken aback by Sevim's neat and beautiful handwriting. There were no errors or crossed-out mistakes. Her tone and the language she used were captivating. It was as if she was listening to the younger self of Sevim sitting next to her. While reading, she even forgot about her surroundings.

Sleeping Simurgh

I WAS HOPELESS OF EVER seeing birds again. In my search, I found many things besides them: a magical path, a secret mountain surrounded by snow. After following clues, walking untaken roads, and the passing of countless days, he was there, under the snow.

The tale I found under the snow that day:

Simurgh opened his eyes after thousands of years of sleep and suddenly shut them. His eyelids were like stones. They were hard to move. A part of him was afraid to see what time had done to the lands around the mountain, but when he opened his eyes again, just for a second, he saw only snow. He couldn't feel the cold, for his head was under his wing, and his wings were so large that Simurgh could imagine he was lost inside them. He did not want to move. A deep unhappiness stirred in his heart, and he did not know why. It had been ages since he had cared about anything. The great bird was like a hen sitting there waiting for her eggs to hatch, although he had none. He did not even care about that. He simply didn't want to move. However, something in him caused his eyes to open again, and this time, he could not close them. Something had changed. The stones that seemed atop his eyelids were getting lighter. Maybe he should try moving his wings a little, "but not yet," he said. For thousands of years, he had not talked with himself either.

Although Simurgh continued to struggle to shut them, the more he tried, the wider his eyes opened. Now, he could see not only was there snow around him, it was also gently snowing. A single snowflake fell upon his back. He was warm under his wings, but as the snowflake melted, he felt its cold spread all around his body. It must have been the first snowflake in millennia that had affected him. "It is not the first time I have seen snow, nor that a snowflake has touched my back," he thought, "Why was that one so important? Its cold flows all through me." He never would know.

His colorful feathers had turned white from being under the snow for so long. His small, black eyes stood out like olives in whiteness. It was easy to see he was a bit worried. His dreams had left him. Again, he tried and could not go back to sleep. The bird felt lonely, and didn't know what to make of it. He had forgotten all the paths, all the roads that once were. He did not know where to go. His memories of Mount Qaf were lost deep inside his mind, just as the mountain was deep in snow. Suddenly, a question fell from his mind to his heart. At once, he forgot about sleep and the dreams he wished to return to and opened his enormous wings for the first time in ages. All the whiteness fell from him at once, revealing his shining feathers. The question began flowing through his blood, and he stood up on his legs to view the mountain. He did not need the past anymore, nevertheless there was only snow.

He called out loudly, hoping somebody would answer, "Where are my birds?!" and heard only his echo. "Where are my birds?!" The questions from his mind kept coming. He could not stop them, "Why haven't they found me? What happened to them?"

He was angry at himself and at his dreams, at the thousands of years that had passed and at the future, at the thundering questions and at the silent responses, at the whiteness and the cold, at the mountain and the sky, and also, at the memories buried beneath the snow. Simurgh wanted to fight with someone, but there was only the snow to fight with, and it was soft, softer than his feathers. He started to walk fast. Maybe he should flex his wings a little, "but not yet," he said to himself. He was also angry at his wings. Why didn't they wake him eons ago? They had covered his head very snuggly, making him warm and comfortable, helping him to indulge in dreams. Part of him wanted to slash his wings as punishment. The great bird was feeling guilty, sad, and also alive.

While walking, he surveyed the mountain. Nothing was familiar. Everything was forgotten. The snow made it harder to remember. From afar, he saw something moving; a wolf's grey tail, a part of a turtle's shell, a fish's head, the one tiny eye of a butterfly, and millions of snowflakes. However, there was no hint of any birds. Had he looked down at the trail left by his talons, he would have seen the tracks of thirty birds imprinted in the snow. Unfortunately, he had not looked.

Only I had seen them, and they were beautiful.

He was awake and very close to me; sad and angry and walking without remembering. However, with his every step, my hope increased.

THE TALE HIS STEPS TOLD me that morning:

One pair of tracks for the leader of the birds, the hoopoe. I was able to hear his call. One pair of tracks for the nightingale, who sang love songs still. One pair of tracks for the parrot with a bright fire that decorated her throat. One pair for the peacock who could entrance a cobra. One pair for the turtledove with the soft coo. One pair for the partridge who strutted with pride. One pair for the hawk who flies on high. One pair for the falcon who wishes no limits to his liberty. The trail of his talons so amazed me that I had almost forgotten about upset Simurgh.

It took maybe one minute, or maybe one day, or perhaps even a year. I wasn't sure. By then, Mount Qaf was covered in his steps. He didn't know how to stop, and nor did he want to. Walking wasn't enough for him.

I thought to myself, "I must calm him down so that he can remember everything he has forgot," only then could I tell him the story of the birds.

"At your feet upon the millions of snowflakes," I shouted, "Look at your talons' trail!" However, he couldn't hear what I said. He wasn't looking at me, unaware that all he needed to do was listen to an ancient story. So, I became silent and patiently followed the tracks, dreaming about the story of his birds. Their song was already in my ears.

Seemingly all at once, the whiteness of the day turned to grey, and the birds' songs left me. It stopped snowing, and a strange wind touched my cheeks. Simurgh had taken to the sky. He was so gorgeous to watch, flying high with his vast wings spread, taking up most of the sky. His shadow covered all as he flew past. I forgot all my worries and wished I could reach up and touch his feathers and fly with him wherever he chose to go. However, it was impossible to catch the majestic bird. He was so far away that he would have to find his story by himself, without my help. The ice in his mind would eventually melt, but when and how?

All Simurgh had left behind was a feather that fell to the ground. Even so, it was so beautiful. While it fell, it danced in the air slowly like a snowflake, putting me under its spell. I picked up the magical plume from where it landed. His feather told me the rest of the story. I was standing in the middle of the trail left by his talons on Mount Qaf. While listening, a thought came to me, "How can I ever leave this place if I don't have wings?"

THE TALE THE FEATHER TOLD me that night:

Simurgh flew all day and night. Before his arduous journey, when he had first flexed his wings, his only thought was of his birds. But as his wings began to flap, he remembered how much he missed flying. At first, he wasn't flying with any particular destination in mind. He just wished to enjoy it. His anger toward his wings quickly subsided, and his mind began to thaw. He flew throughout the Earth, never looking back, not stopping to rest or perching anywhere. After thousands of years of sleep, he felt happy and relaxed. He had been reborn. Now, nothing could make him go back to sleep. What he was witnessing now was better than his dreams. He was racing with the sun and moon. As the sun rose in the East, he was already in the West. In the dark, his feathers radiated brighter than moonlight. He missed the cold of Mount Qaf and would miss it even more later.

That night, the people who looked up at the sky saw a brilliant star above their heads. Some thought it was a shooting star and immediately made a wish. What they wished was accepted instantly. Some of them thought it was the devil and were scared to death. Yet they were lucky, for nobody died that night. However, most people failed to look at the sky. So, they continued their miserable lives without being aware of anything. In some lands, it was cloudy and raining, and in some, there was snow. In some, there was war. Some were already forgotten since their cities and towns had been destroyed or abandoned long ago. But Simurgh had no thoughts of any of that. He was still enjoying his flight. He started to imagine that he was approaching his hiding birds with each flap of his wings. He had no idea that birds had become extinct; nobody had seen even a part of a wing, beak, or talon for decades. Owls' bright eyes were not opening during the night, bluebirds were not singing, and eggs were not hatching.

Many sunrises and sunsets had passed by. The great bird's memory seemed like a puzzle, with all its pieces in a scattered mess. Everything was shattered. The land, though now different, was unmistakably familiar. As the memories slowly started to reassemble, a scene from an old city came into Simurgh's mind. He recalled birds, unique and vibrant, zipping through its narrow alleys. Something in that ancient city was calling, and soon, he found the very place spread out before him. Drawn to this ancient city, he slowed his beating wings, yielding to gravity.

Hovering above, he surveyed the narrow strait, splitting the town into two: West on one side, East on the other. To the south, the waterway met a turquoise sea; to the north, it stretched to a somber black watery expanse. This city, now known as Dar us Saadat, had bore many names over the ages. Yet, amidst their hectic lives, its inhabitants had forgotten the meaning of 'saadat.' They'd rise before the sun and labor until fatigue claimed them, lamenting, "Once, this city was different." Some whispered it was as ancient as the Earth itself, yet its beauty remained undiminished, ever captivating, like a blossoming spring flower.

Amid the strait's frenzy of boats, Simurgh paused and rested in its flow, looking around to see if he could find any birds. The current cityscape clashed with his fractured memories. Gone were the quaint wooden houses, replaced by towering, grim stone structures that cloaked the land in shadows. The once-clear air was now thick with an alien smoky haze. Harsh shouts and curses punctuated the loud ambient noise. It was painful to look at the anguish. Even the strait was too congested, from nimble boats darting past massive ships carrying goods to warships carefully navigating their way through. Oblivious to Simurgh's presence, they weaved a frenetic dance of near misses. The scene overwhelmed him, and he felt dizzy. Nevertheless, he scanned the ship's decks, the rooftops, the fishermen's nets, and even amongst the shoes of the people along the water's banks but found no trace of birds. Unbeknownst to him, his majestic talons had left a trail behind.

A potent aroma of coffee wafted from a nondescript, narrow alley. Drawn inexplicably to it, Simurgh darted into the city's heart, desperate to escape the maritime chaos. However, the urban labyrinth proved even more confounding. Narrow, twisting streets stretched endlessly, with stalls displaying their myriad goods. The fish's pungent scent clashed with heady spices, overwhelming the comforting coffee aroma. Vendors called out, and people hurried by—everyone seemingly in a chase for something. Pearls gleamed beside sweet treats. As Simurgh tried to regain his balance, a gust whirled by, lifting headdresses and shawls alike.

"Look at all this bedlam! What's going on?" shouted a man.

Navigating the tight streets became an ordeal for Simurgh. Carriages sped by, their wheels threatening his talons. An awning from a tall building grazed him, leaving a gash on his cheek. Blood, stark against his plumage, dripped down, each droplet narrating a silent tale of his distress. He didn't know it, but he was the only bird left on Earth. One drop of blood fell upon a stone. One drop of blood fell into the grass. One drop of blood fell down through a maintenance hole into the underground of the city.

The great bird was miserable and upset even more than he was when he first awoke on Mouth Qaf.

No one seemed even to take notice of him, let alone see his despair. No one except a blind beggar at the corner of the street. He shouted, "Simurgh is here!"

Nobody heard his cry except the street cats and dogs resting beside him. A white cat licked her lips. A black dog shook his tail, and the rest of them kept sleeping. A woman conversing with her friend walked by and tossed a single coin to the blind beggar without bothering to listen or look.

Simurgh's steps slowed, and he almost wished to return to the mountain and sleep another millennium. For the first time since the beginning of his long journey, he stopped and rested right there between the street cats and dogs. He searched the flowers' leaves that hung along the buildings' balconies and walls and the corny foods atop the street peddlers' carts. There was no sign to the whereabouts of any birds. Then a cat, with one eye that was colored blue and the other yellow-golden, saw the giant bird. But instead of being scared away, it came next to the Simurgh, cuddled amongst the feathers of one of his wings, and fell instantly asleep. The wing was comfortable, and the cat had a lovely nap.

The Sleeping Lilith

THE THIRD DROP OF SIMURGH'S blood that had fallen into the underground had landed and started to flow through the sewer lines. It passed many hungry rats' whiskers and many cracks. It finally came to a stop deep down in a silent and still cavern where it expected to dry up and be forever lost. What it did not know was that it had stopped very close to a witch who had been asleep, hidden in that cave for centuries. Her white hair was so long and unruly that it covered her whole body, even her naked, hobbled feet. The whole mess made it impossible to see her eyes. But if you could have looked carefully, you might have been able to make out her thin, dry lips under all of it. There was not part of her skin that wasn't wrinkled. She was so ugly that the snakes stayed away and did not dare to taste her, nor the famished rats. When the strong smell of Simurgh's drop of blood reached her, she opened her eyes suddenly. Her body was thin and weak, but her mind was crystal clear. She hadn't forgotten even a second of her life from before. She knew the past, and from the prophecies, she knew some of the future.

She took a deep breath, exhaled slowly, and quickly took another, relishing every second. The witch didn't know where the blood was, but with her strong sense of smell, she followed its scent, wriggling towards it like a snake because she could not yet walk. Her thin lips smiled as she got closer, her heart racing. She carefully moved her right hand so as not to disperse and ruin the drop, touched it with her fingertip, and put it to her tongue. As soon as she tasted it, she understood that Simurgh had awoke and risen. She felt strength return to her limbs as the great bird's blood healed her. She wanted more—needed more, not the blood, but Simurgh himself. He could bring her what she required amongst the world's far-off, secret places. She got up slowly, started walking, and found her way back up to the surface.

While listening, I wanted to burn the feather then and there to try and end the tale forever.

"Can you stop, please!" I begged the feather, "Why don't you tell me a different tale?"

"What is wrong?" it asked calmly.

"He doesn't need a witch! She is going to hurt him. Change the story!"

"Nothing can change it, and don't worry."

"Are you from a vulture?"

"Stop complaining and listen."

She popped her head up from a maintenance hole in the center of a street and immediately started looking around for the bird. She was so excited her legs began to shake. The old woman had missed the fresh air, the sounds of the street, and the colors of the sky.

It was easy for her to find Simurgh. He was still there, beside the blind beggar, between the alley cats and dogs. He was trying to think of a way to fill his feelings of emptiness from the absence of other birds. Every now and then since he had arrived, he would fly up onto one of the many roofs and jump between them, looking for any sign of them. Or he would fly over the sea and dive down to catch some fish for himself and the cats. One of the cats had newborn kittens, six in all. Simurgh kept an eye out for them from the competing rats. The kittens' eyes and ears were still shut, just drinking milk from their mother and sleeping. Their helplessness reminded Simurgh of himself and his quest to find his lost birds.

The witch came and sat next to them. Nobody had yet noticed her, not even the blind beggar. That was what she wanted. She wasn't ready to talk with Simurgh yet. He had the power to kill her, or, maybe worse, he might just fly away forever. She knew how frightening she must seem to others. How could she make Simurgh believe her? She picked up one of the fish, which the cats hadn't eaten yet, and started gnawing on it. She was hungry after being asleep all those years. It was hard to chew, but she liked the taste of it.

The witch waited until well after midnight when all the restaurants and cafes had closed, and the streets were empty and quiet. Even the blind beggar had gotten up and left his corner. The boats were still, with their captains in deep sleep and their crews snoring. Fish were dancing under the sea in the moonlight, and an old song was being sung from an open window somewhere. A woman's crying could be heard coming from a faraway bench. Dry leaves were falling on top of the sleeping kittens. The only souls awake there were Simurgh and the witch. And they were not looking at each other.

Simurgh was staring up at the sky. There were so many stars. He imagined them as his birds, flying in a flock up so high, looking for him. Maybe he shouldn't have left the mountain. Perhaps he should have stayed there forever, not moving a feather, or maybe he should fly somewhere else. But he had become attached to the street corner with the kittens. Simurgh had gotten past the anxiety of the crowds around there in the morning, the blind beggar, and the ships in the sea.

The witch was sitting on the edge of a short, knee-high wall that ran along the shore abutting the water, with her legs hanging over the end and her feet soaking in the sea. She had tried her best to tie up her hair, but it wasn't easy. There was just too much of it. She looked at her feet and the small fish swimming under them. The moonlight was just enough for her sharp eyes to see well; she could see excellently in the dark. From the reflections off the dark waters, she caught glimpses of her face. She saw her dry lips, her wrinkled skin, and glittering green eyes like two holes filled with green fireflies. They were so bright even she was surprised. The last time she had seen herself was hundreds of years ago. She had forgotten. Her eyes had always glowed like that, even when she was young. A fish broke the surface of the still water near her feet with a splash, breaking the image of her face and waking her from her thoughts.

She stood up. Her skirt was a little bit wet, and so were her feet. The old woman started to walk with one hand in her pocket towards Simurgh, who was still gazing at the sky above. In her pocket was a collection of magical stones that she started carefully fidgeting with between her fingers. She walked right in front of the bird. Simurgh tore his eyes away from the sky and looked straight into her glittering eyes. The witch stared back.

He was confused. "Who are you?"

"I wish I could say 'an old friend,' but we never met."

"What are you doing here?"

"Nothing. Just fiddling with my stones." And the witch slowly took out her hand from her pocket and showed him the stones.

"Don't you think it's too late to play games?"

"It is not a game. It's magic." She cast the stones down upon the sidewalk, and they stopped rolling next to the sleeping kittens. Simurgh saw five or six small rocks and a strange light between them. "A sorcerer taught me that many, many years ago. I like to use them when I'm lost. It shows me 'ways.' Old ways and new ways. Right ones and wrong ones. The ways to find things that are lost. You look like you're lost too."

"I'm not lost," said Simurgh nervously.

"What about your birds? Don't you want to find them?"

"Do you know where they are?" Simurgh stood up on his legs, surprised.

"I wish I knew. But I can help you find them." She picked up the stones and cast them one more time. Again, they rolled to a stop next to the sleeping kittens. Simurgh was confused. Where should he look for the answer to how he could find his birds? At the light from her eyes or the light between the stones. It was dark and hard to see her face in the alley. Why should he believe her? But then he started to see it and how to get there. The witch's finger, moving slowly, traced its path between the stones.

"Your past is under the snow," she said. "There is only one way I know to melt through it and find the birds." Again, she moved her finger amongst the stones. "You need to fly..." She took a long breath, "West! There is a mountain there. Not huge, not small. I see an ocean not too far from it. Many rocks, much sand and snow." She was talking fast, and Simurgh, so excited, listening to every word, could barely breathe. "There is also a lake next to it. A very special one. You need to find the lake and bring me a drop of its water, and I will be able to give you your birds." She gave him an empty bottle and plucked a feather from him without asking.

"What are you doing!?" Simurgh was angry.

"I need one of your feathers too. While you fly to the lake, I will prepare my potion. It will be ready when you come back."

"Why should I believe you?" He looked at her eye sockets of fireflies once more but couldn't find any trickery in them. Without waiting for an answer, he flexed his wings and took to the sky. As he rose, he turned his head to look back at her and shouted, "Take care of those kittens. No one should touch them. I will soon return."

The witch watched him, and as he flew away, dawn broke. Her wrinkled face was smiling.

"It's not the end, right?" I asked.

"No, it's not the end," said the feather.

"Would you please tell me more?"

"Yes, I will. But not right now." said the feather.

I waited and waited. The feather was silent. I walked around the mountain. The snow had started to melt under the sun, revealing some small flowers that poked up here and there. I couldn't wait anymore and once more asked the feather, "What is the rest of the tale?" So, it spoke.

"No one should touch them," the witch mumbled Simurgh's last words. What the bird didn't know was that she hated cats. She knew many potions that used a cat's blood or a piece of a cat's tail. Kittens were especially useful for some kinds of magic too. A newborn kitten's eyes were great for bait. With only the eye of a kitten, she could have caught a magical fish swimming through the city's strait. With that old fish's oil, she could prepare a youth potion and, perhaps, make herself beautiful again. With a cat's ear, she could have made delicious food to enchant the people. One bite of it, and they would obey her every word. "But anyways," she said to herself, "I'm not going to touch them. I will take care of the kittens until Simurgh returns. What he's bringing me is more important and valuable than any magic." She was upset, and her hands started to itch.

Most of the morning, she sat beside the cats and the dogs in the corner, watching the street. She used that afternoon to prepare the potion for Simurgh. She picked up some black moss from a shallow place beside the shore. She found a yellow tulip and a grey rose in a public garden. With Simurgh's feather, now she just needed a drop of the lake's water.

"I hope he won't be too long," the witch muttered.

Flying West was easy for Simurgh. This time, he didn't watch the sun or the moon rise or set, nor did he care whether it was day or night. His mind was only on the destination. Soon, he found himself next to the ocean the witch had shown him. He saw sunken ships, broken shells, and dead starfish along its coasts, but he didn't waste time on these. He flew to the mountains and forests close by to find the lake. However, it wasn't that easy.

There were so many lakes, and the witch didn't exactly tell him which was the special one. He flew from one lake to the next. Some were full of fish, and others were only full of rocks. But none were magical. He searched all of them—every single one.

"Should I go back and ask the witch which specific lake she meant?" he wondered.

The majestic bird soared past bridges, giant trees, and tall waterfalls. Then, a bird song filled his ears. He wasn't expecting that. Excited, he followed the song, and then the lake was there. He came close to the water's edge, and when he looked into it, he saw his birds under the water. Instantly, he dove into the lake to free them, but underwater he found nothing. The lake seemed to be a strange sort of cage, trapping them inside. Or perhaps, was the lake's surface just a mirror showing what was trapped inside of him? He sat still as a statue, staring at them so intensely that he didn't even blink. Then the bird remembered what the witch had said and the bottle she had given him. He filled it with the lake's water and took off, rushing back as fast as he could fly.

When Simurgh returned to the alley corner, he saw the witch holding one of the kittens. As soon as she saw him, she sneezed.

"I am allergic to cats," she cried, "and this cat is sick! He hasn't eaten anything since you've been gone! I don't know what to do!" And then she saw the bottle, "Oh! You found it," she exclaimed.

Simurgh was silent.

"Here are your kittens! Nobody hurt them, not even me! Give the bottle to me and wait here. I need some time. I will come back soon." She took the bottle and left.

She came back at night, this time holding two bottles, one for Simurgh and one for herself.

Simurgh asked, "Why do you have two bottles?"

"One of them is for me. I want to live longer, and that potion will help," the old woman smiled, "Possibly, I will miss this corner," she stated. Then, she took one sip of the bottle and disappeared!

Simurgh took one sip from the bottle and immediately vanished!

And, in his place, thirty of his birds reappeared and flew away, scattering in all directions. People asleep woke immediately when they heard their long, absent songs. With every flap of their wings, more and more birds appeared from each of them. They all flew around the world, spreading out and returning to the world. And since then, you can find a bird in every tree.

One flew near me and whispered, "It's the end."

IT WAS STILL NIGHT WHEN Azra finished reading the story, but the candles had burned down low, threatening to go out. While closing the book, a feather fell to the ground, dazzling Azra's eyes.

The next day, she knocked on Sevim's door. The feather and the notebook were in her hands.

When the old lady opened it, she said, "I knew you would visit as soon as the sun rose. You are such an impatient girl. Come in, come in," and she opened the door widely. Sevim seemed rested and more energetic.

When they sat down, Sevim started talking without pausing to take questions. "I wrote it because I didn't want to forget even the smallest detail, which was a good idea. Let me tell you, the feather has never spoken since."

Azra spoke for the first time, "I couldn't believe you wrote this! How many years ago did it happen? Nobody's ever spoken anything about this before."

Sevim paused to remember and answered, "It should have been around forty years ago. You weren't even born yet."

Azra asked another, "You said the witch prepared a potion using Simurgh's feather. Maybe we bring the sea back with the feather you have hidden." She touched the feather and gazed at it, hoping to learn something.

"They say the feather of the Simurgh is full of healing. That's the reason why I spoke with you yesterday and why I gave you my book. Aegean will return, but it won't be easy," Sevim murmured.

For the first time in a long while, Azra felt a lightness on her and prayed for the waves to return.

CHAPTER FOUR

The Ashes of the Forest

NOTHING WAS THE SAME. EVERYTHING was dry in the village. Only the salt stayed, and on sunny days the surface of the pebbles still kept shining like in the old days. Without the whispers and songs of Aegean Sea, the joy left the people as if it had gone forever. She took her ancient legends and vanished. Nobody believed it at first. The sargo fish, sand eels, and octopuses were missing. Despair and pain remained. The situation got worse with the forest fire. Not even a tiny raindrop fell to the ground, and the flames became wilder until whatever it could take from the forest, it took. The branches of the olive trees turned black. The tongue of the flames came closer to the village, but luckily, it couldn't touch the houses or trees inside of it. Only a cloud of dark smoke swirled around slowly like a thief. It wrapped around Azra's neck and left her breathless. There was no sign of life in the branches of Azra's fig tree, but she was waiting for the day when it would bloom again when the weather started to warm up. A wind began to blow, mixing the dead trees' ashes together with the dry inlet's salt. And then the wind started wandering around recklessly, with a low hum.

Azra preferred not to open the curtains. She didn't want to see the hungry frames, the dark, smoky sky, or the abandoned inlet. She was scared, and at night, she covered her body with a thick blanket, imagining herself under the sea. She felt powerless and breathless there, but its deep coolness made it seem safer. She still possessed the feather of Simurgh, the black moss, and Elmados' ship. But what could she do with them, "Nothing," she murmured. The wind began knocking on Azra's door with its ashes and sea salt. She heard its hums. After a long while, she finally opened the curtains, and her eyes were overwhelmed by the destitution they took in.

Then she saw her younger self when she was a child in the empty street. Her curly, honey brown hair covered her face, but she was undeniably smiling and twirling around while singing. She was wearing her favorite yellow dress with miniature fruit patterns embroidered on it, with a white ribbon around her waist. The younger Azra stopped and saw her older self through the window. Between them was a garden surrounded by a short, white fence and some leafless flowers. For a while, they both just stared at each other. The smile on the little girl's face vanished, and her lips froze. Her brown eyes peered through her long bangs hanging in front of them. As the youth opened her mouth to say something to the woman behind the window, she vanished. What would the young girl have said to Azra? The older woman would never know. But she remembered fondly the yellow dress she used to wear. When the image of the youth disappeared, the street was deserted again.

Azra could see the white houses around her. Most of them were empty. Their windows and doors were tightly shut, with the wooden shutters remaining open, swaying in the wind. Almost all of the villagers had left. She had only her memories to fill the streets. Laughter, children's songs *–come out, let's play–*a mother's angry voice *–come to dinner now!* Azra's old uncle greeting her as he passed by her garden, the neighbor who came to invite her for tea. Now, they were all in the past. Across the street, the old olive tree yet stood. It would still give plenty to eat in the fall. Azra called it "The Blind One" because someone had carved two shut eyes on its trunk with a pocket knife. Those eyes would never open.

While closing the curtains, she thought of the Pearl Seller. He had been collecting the sea's legends for years. Maybe he would know what to do, and she quickly resolved to find him. For that, she would have to jump over the marble fence again. No matter what happened, Azra was going to talk with him. She couldn't just sit at home all day and watch the dance of fire and smoke in the distance. She washed her face, hastily braided her hair, put on a red sweater and her wool hat, and left her house practically running.

Some paths are not easy to walk. Not because of the gravel or brushes. Not because of the mysterious sounds you hear before each step. Azra knew there wasn't some wild animal or a monster waiting to eat her. It was not the first time she had traveled this trail. She had done it once before when Elmados was here. But since then, everything had changed. The unknown possibilities at the end of it scared her, and she wasn't ready to hear what the Pearl Seller had to say. However, Simurgh's feather gave her hope. Azra was most afraid that when she reached the end of the pathway, her hopes would die. What if the Pearl Seller commanded, "Go away!" or proclaimed, "There is nothing I can do?" But there was another possibility. He would whisper into her ears a lost legend he might remember about the feather, for he was very knowledgeable of such things. With this thought, Azra became excited.

She stood in front of the old marble wall on the north side of the village and stared at the yellow sign that had "Blind Alley" written on it. Then, succumbing to an old habit, she turned her face towards the sea. It hurt not being able to hear the sounds of the waves. She tried to imagine the old man she had come to see sitting in his home. Eventually, Azra jumped over the wall. The trees were black on the other side of the marble fence, or what was left of them after the fire.

Her steps were slow. "Perhaps, I should go back home," she said while remembering her cozy blanket and the thick curtains where she felt safe. But the dead trees and the smoke she felt in her lungs kept her moving. Then, Azra noticed movement. Something was there in the woods. Peeking at the noise through the gaps of the burnt, leafless trunks, a shapeless creature appeared and was heading towards Azra. Was it a man or an animal? Was it something that would hurt her? She froze, her heart racing. She tried forcing herself to shout, "Who's there?" but, nevertheless, couldn't move her lips. As it got closer, the formless shadow turned into a man, an older man, the Pearl Seller. Azra took a deep breath, and her heartbeats returned to normal. She hadn't expected to meet him here. Without thinking, she started to walk toward him. What was he doing here? He never came to meet with anybody from the village. What had happened to him?

"Hi," they said at the same time.

"How are..." The same words came out of their mouths and mixed with each other's. They paused and smiled. A gust blew down from above and whipped up the fallen ashes, swirling them into the air around them. The silence from the absent waves tugged at their hearts.

"I was coming to see you. Probably you can guess why," said Azra while touching the darkened branches with her fingertips.

The man whom Azra had last seen many months ago was not the same. Even though he didn't say anything, his face showed he was tired and worried. His eyes were wide open, confused, and eager to learn anything. He wore a gray vest with a thick scarf around his neck. His white hair was a mess. Who knows how long it had been since he had trimmed his beard? It was as if he had just recovered from a long, severe illness. Yet, wasn't this also the mysterious man who possessed thousands of stories and had sold hundreds of pearls taken from the depths of the sea? And because of it, perhaps the wealthiest man around. It was only a year since she first visited his house, yet it now seemed like centuries ago.

"Let's walk to the shore," he said, "we can sit there."

Silence accompanied their steps, with only the soft crunch of pebbles under their feet. They had come to the right arm of the inlet to the Mossy Village, the part facing the sea near the village. They were near five tiny houses built parallel to the shore, yet still outside the village. The old scenic view of the sea now looked over a flat abandoned wasteland without waves or much water. Small stones and dry sea moss covered the area. In the distance was an old pier. It was so rusty that if someone were to touch it, they would cut their hand so that it bled. Its baseboards had been dismantled, and only its skeleton remained. It looked like a strange, forgotten scarecrow in this place without the sea. Azra saw a couple of chairs, their fabric blowing in the wind. The villagers would sit and talk for hours there. But the benches still looked sound. A dog barked in the distance when the call to prayer began from the mosque behind the trees. Both stopped speaking as it echoed across the wasteland. There was no one else other than them. Someone new would not believe that once people swam here in joy. The blue of the sea looked far away, as if it was a distant mountain range. It seemed it would take a day's journey to reach. Azra missed what the waves would bring her.

"My life is almost spent. I can feel it," the Pearl Seller proclaimed. "This dry shore is a portent of my own death." He stopped talking for a while and coughed. Then he continued, "The smoke hurts my lungs! I hope it rains soon. I never thought I would see you again. You were angry at me because of what I said to you. What happened to Elmados?"

Azra said, "He left."

"You should be happy now."

"Well," Azra said. She couldn't look into the Pearl Seller's eyes. "It was good for him. He probably found himself a ship and is traveling around the world in search of his answer," she said and looked up at the seagulls flying above them. Forgotten waves stirred in the Pearl Seller's blue eyes. The old man seemed to be hiding the sea within.

"Don't worry. Elmados might return," he said. "Anyways, why did you want to talk with me?"

"Why were you headed to the village. I've never seen you go there. You're always busy with your pearls and customers."

"I was," he admitted. He picked up a small stick from the ground and used it to poke and play with the sand as young boys often do. "I was consumed with grief. I lost my wife, and my kids have left to faraway shores. I don't know if they shall ever return. They are roamers like I was. But I stayed at home and sold my pearls. It's the only way I've found to bear my sorrow and sadness. However," he sighed deeply and stared at the abandoned shore "now everything has changed. In my time, I've met many people and traveled from island to island. My old eyes have seen numerous lands. In some, I stayed only a day. In others, I desired to stay much longer. I've seen many unexplained things. But I've never seen the sea go so far out. At first, I thought it was just a strange tide. Then, of course, she would return. But, no! She almost vanished!" The Pearl Seller raised his voice and stared into Azra's face. He pointed out towards the horizon with his hand. "Aegean is far over there! How will I live without her next to me? My old eyes look forward to seeing her as soon as the morning starts. My ears are attuned to her waves. Now there's only an empty ringing in them. I was wondering how you were doing. Maybe we can find some way to fix this together."

Azra remembered the feather in her pocket but didn't take it out.

First, she wanted to tell how she had come to possess it and asked the old man, "Have you ever heard the name Sevim?"

The Pearl Seller shook his head as if to say no.

Azra reached into her pocket and touched the feather once more. Her voice trembled with excitement, "An old lady, Sevim, told me that once upon a time before I was born, the birds had vanished from the world. She said our black moss in the sea captured her and took her to Mount Qaf to meet with Simurgh. She doesn't know why the sea has left, but she thought it would help, so she gave me..."

Azra took the feather out of her pocket and showed it to him. It was colorful and shined in front of them. The old man had never seen anything like it before. "She gave me this. Long ago, the waves brought her to Simurgh. Sevim believes that we can bring them back."

The Pearl Seller gazed at the feather in silence. Then he spoke, "'A feather from his wing summoned turmoil.' I read this on an epitaph many years ago: 'As he fluttered in the sky, those who struggled to catch his shadow on the earth only multiplied turmoil and led people to disaster. Those who could see him buried his secret for eternity." He smiled as he placed one hand on his chin and gently touched the feather with the other, "I never imagined it would suddenly appear before me like this. This feather belongs to Simurgh. I was skeptical when those familiar with it said I would recognize it immediately, but I was wrong."

"Have you ever seen the bird?" asked Azra eagerly.

"No, never," said the Pearl Seller. "However, I've heard much of him and his feathers, particularly on an island I visited once. Oh, I was young then," He ruffled his white hair, "Let's walk to the sea." He got up and brushed the dry sand off his legs. Azra was confused. Since the waves had left, she had never thought of walking out along the deserted shore. She was used to swimming there, not walking.

The old man laughed while walking through the vast dry beach.

"Oh, all the memories hidden here. When I was a child, I was afraid of the sea. I remember when I first learned how to swim. Later, I brought my kids here and taught them how to speak with Aegean. It's so odd that the water is gone. I've always wondered what was hidden in the deep parts. I guess that's one reason I became a sailor and traveled. What I saw of it was never enough. I always wanted more."

Azra was listening with admiration. She had never traveled far offshore from the Mossy Village and had never dived into the deep parts of the sea. The starfish field might have been the farthest she had gone out. The sun was going down, and the clouds had started to turn pink. Their two tiny shadows moved between the black moss. It was as if they were in a labyrinth whose walls were made from it, impossible to escape from for a stranger who didn't know. However, Azra and the Pearl Seller knew this part of the sea well. Both of them had grown up on this shore, and they could find their way even in darkness.

At first, the smell of iodine mixed with the smell of dead fish amongst the moss and made it difficult to breathe. However, after a couple of minutes, their noses became used to it, and the pungent smell became tolerable. From a distance, they looked like a father and daughter or a master with his pupil.

They found a piece of a child's shoe, its brown leather turned black, with green moss covering it. And a rotted, forgotten part of cloth peeking out from underneath the sand. A crooked, rusted knife. Some worthless coins. Thousands of urchins and sea shells could be found everywhere.

The Pearl Seller plucked out a piece of dry moss and said, "Damn stuff. You can't imagine how many times it kept me from sailing out. It wraps around the keel and won't let you go. It's a nightmare, but you can learn how to use it to great advantage. For that, you absolutely need experience, years and years.

"Oh, how I was young and inexperienced then when I came to the island where I learned of the legends of Simurgh and many other things. Then, I was obsessed with finding pearls. And my passion for discovering them and getting rich was my dearest dream. The only one I wanted to talk with was Aegean. I had a crew with me, and we were sailing where Aegean meets the Mediterranean. There are the straits to the rest of the world. Nothing would stop me from sailing through them. But it started with a cursed plant wrapping around the hull that refused to let go. We tried cutting the damn stuff away, but it still came back! It was impossible. Day by day, more and more of it shrouded the ship and started to weigh us down. Until it ultimately sank us." The Pearl Seller stopped to catch his breath. They were still walking out to the sea.

Azra asked, "Do you want to finish your story later? We can go back to the shore now if you wish."

The old man shook his head, "No," he rearranged a bunch of black moss he had been gathering as they went so that he could carry it better.

The girl and the old man kept walking as he continued, "I couldn't do anything for my comrade. He drowned right next to me. His name was Mustafa. He left behind two children and a woman. It was all my fault—the cursed plant came because of my greed. I saw my own death approaching, and I would have met it with Mustafa if not for some moss that suddenly snarled around my feet and carried me to that island. Moss just like this." He held up the bunch in his hand. "It left me unconscious, lying on its shore. I was awakened by hands that had grasped me by my shoulders and started pulling. My eyes were shut, but I could hear the sound of the sand beneath me while I was dragged. Just for a moment, I was able to force my eyes open and saw a brown figure, a man. His back was turned to me. And then I passed out again."

The Pearl Seller paused and looked at Azra, "Let's start heading back. It's getting late."

The last rays of the sun were fading and left the surroundings darkened. The labyrinth of black moss in the dim light looked uncanny.

He continued the story as they walked back, "When I awoke, my eyes opened upon a dungeon. After Mustafa's death, I deserved it. For days afterward, every morning at sunrise, a monk in a brown woolen cloak came to my cell and passed me some food. I only ever saw his mouth, which he never used, from under his hood. He held a lantern as he walked to help light his way in the dark passageway outside the cell. Eventually, one day, he took out a bunch of keys and, with one of them, opened my door. It was then that I first heard his voice. It wasn't friendly.

"He ordered, 'Come,' and took me to their head abbot. After climbing many stairs, we arrived at the abbot's room. The abbot wore the same brown cloak as the monk but had a red belt and a white beard.

"'Too much ambition for a small ship,' he chastised. 'And if you're not careful, you'll lose even more than that, including your soul. You may stay here as long as you don't disturb the island's inhabitants. Spent some time here and rest. Perhaps build a new ship if you wish. I know we haven't treated you very nicely. However, from now on, you'll see our hospitality.'

The Pearl Seller continued, "The abbot never called on me again. All the islanders were monks, and they worked in silence. I would hear only the rustling of their clothes, footsteps going up and down the stairs, and doors opening and closing. If I made the slightest noise, one of their hands would dart out from under the brown cloak, reach their lips, and warn me, 'Hush!'"

Azra and the Pearl Seller came to the old shoreline and gathered some driftwood. The old man was tired and stopped talking. With the wood, he started a fire. After the fire reached a nice size, he carefully placed the dry moss on top of it.

For a moment, nothing happened. And then, a great burst of sparks and flames leapt into the air above and swirled around, forming a giant blaze of orange, green, and blue. At the center of the now great bonfire appeared the image of Simurgh flapping his wings.

Staring into the flames, the old man whispered, "I'll tell you the rest of the story later."

The Crooked Paths

THREE DAYS LATER...

On the morning Azra visited the Pearl Seller, she sat on an overturned, half-rotting boat staring towards the abandoned shore. She was surrounded by other derelict rowboats. The many oars of these wrecks were scattered about here and there. Before Aegean Sea had left the coast, all these vessels had wandered aimlessly in the salty water. Azra couldn't believe that a year ago, the village fishermen were sailing far out as the fishing season had arrived. Those who wanted to stay closer chased snapper, bream, and sardines, patiently wandering along the shoreline.

As the sea had receded day by day, all the villagers had migrated to other towns that jutted further out to stay closer to the new coastline. Azra didn't blame them. They didn't know how to live on dry land. When she was a child, she used to play hide-and-seek, and between beached, wrecked boats like these was her favorite place to hide. But now, she didn't feel any joy. It was like sitting in a graveyard of forgotten memories.

WHILE SITTING ON AN OVERTURNED boat, Azra remembered the screams Aegean had brought her. Those unfamiliar with the salty waters and the mystery of the black moss could easily drown off the coast of the Mossy Village, coming perilously close to death. Aegean always behaved wildly in their bay; even a skilled swimmer could drown along the village's shores. Azra would run without hesitation when she heard cries for help from the shore.

Once, she dove into the water and saw two hands struggling in the open sea, begging to be rescued. Now, as she stared at the emptiness left by the sea, those cries echoed in her ears once more. That time when approaching the drowning man, she noticed a speargun in his hand. With deadly stubbornness, he refused to release it, risking that, with the slightest mistake, he could accidentally shoot her.

Azra had shouted in panic, "Drop your spear. Otherwise, I can't save you!" Eventually, he dropped it, but pulling him ashore was not easy. When they finally got there, he was still breathless, and his chest was moving in and out so fast. The salty water dripped from his light brown hair into his face. The man was young, but Azra couldn't guess his age.

While trying to breathe, he said, "I don't know what happened to me. I've caught numerous fish spearfishing; dentex, tuna, and groupers, but today, something happened to me out there. The black moss caught my foot while I was swimming through it." He closed his eyes for a while, trying to rest. One of his feet was bleeding, probably because of the urchins' needles he had stepped on. The blood mixed with the salty water on his body and ran down amongst the stones where he was lying. His breathing started to slow down.

The fisherman opened his eyes and stood up, "My spear! I can't lose it. I paid a fortune for it and can't afford another one." Without even looking back at Azra, he started to search for it along the shore. The dark blue waves were not high then.

"It can't sink," Azra said, "It should be floating on the surface somewhere." She saw a silhouette that matched a little further away and shouted in a hurry, "It's there!"

They dove into the sea and tried to catch up with the spear, but the closer the two young swimmers swam towards it, the farther out it went. Aegean took the spear away from them and sent it to another one of its coasts. By then, the sun was setting, and the sky was getting dark. The waves ceased, and Aegean turned as flat as a lake. They had gone out far away from the shore before they gave up. While they swam back to the beach, Azra could see the black moss under her. The long black leaves were dancing in the current and trying to catch her feet.

Arriving back to shore, they were both so frustrated that they didn't dare to talk for a while. The sun had already set. Purple clouds were moving slowly over the peak of Mount Ida in the distance. The spear fisherman stared at Aegean, still in shock.

After a long wait, he said, "I almost died. How can I thank you?" Then, pausing as if remembering something, he continued, "Have you ever heard of an underwater field of starfish? One day, I'll take you there. We'll go before I've even bought a new spear."

Azra was quiet. She was a bit upset that she hadn't heard about that place like that. She'd seen many things under the sea but never a place full of starfish.

"What is your name?" he asked,

"Azra."

By that time, her body was shivering from the cold. She turned and started to run back home without even saying, "Goodbye."

He shouted back, "Next week, on Thursday, I'll take you to the starfish field!" he added, "Be ready to swim! I hope you're a good swimmer."

She shouted back, "No doubt, I'm a good swimmer. I saved your life!"

Azra had seen fields of colorful mussels and dead urchins' shells beneath the waves. She had her own collection of them, but not starfish. They were so rare. Sometimes Aegean brought her one, but they were always dead and alone, and their arms were always broken. She had never seen a field full of starfish, nor even one alive.

Azra told her friend Fatima about the drowning spear fisherman while Fatima was braiding her own hair. She asked, "Did you get his name?"

"No."

Fatima looked back at her from under her messy black hair, and said, "Instead of meeting with him in the middle of the mysterious Aegean, you should meet with him in the town square and have some fun."

Azra searched for her green eyes under her hair and said, "I always go into town, but I've never seen a field of live starfish." She was getting angry but subdued it and added, "Why don't you come with us?"

"Perhaps," Fatima murmured back, adding, "He wants to save money for a new harpoon. Otherwise, he would have gone into town with you." She smiled as she tied the end of her braid.

AZRA, FATIMA, AND A FEW other friends met the swimmer the following Thursday. They swam through the secret paths of the sea. Azra had never gone that far out from the Mossy Village. When she turned around and looked at it, their houses were small white dots along the shore. She couldn't tell fig trees from olives, and the vast mountain range in the distance towered over the village. She looked beneath her and saw that the sea had become much deeper and its color had darkened. The black moss was untouchable here. They seemed like shadows in the depths.

Maybe she should have swum back, but the spear fisherman called out, "Hey, don't stop now! We still have far to go."

They swam past unfamiliar things; unknown villages poked out of the shore in the distance. Eventually, they came to the starfish field. Azra's eyes started to burn when she opened them under salty water. Still, it was worth it when, in the blurry water, she saw hundreds of red and yellow starfish along the bottom. They were moving slowly. She wanted to dive down and pick up one, but she couldn't hold her breath and go down so deep. The swimmer quickly dove to the bottom and grabbed a red one. When he returned to the surface, he laughed and placed the starfish on Azra's shoulder. In the sunlight, it shone. It felt like needles were pricking her burning eyes because of the salt, but it didn't matter. The starfish's arm slowly moved about and tickled her skin. She took that starfish back with her.

A couple of hours later, the swimmers arrived back to land again. Ashore, the starfish had become lethargic. Azra guessed it was dying.

"Return it to the sea, or it will die," said one of the swimmers as they bid farewell to their friends.

"No, it's mine," said Azra. "Aegean can't take it from me."

At night, it stopped moving and died. Its color became brown, and its outer skin changed to a dull shell. She placed it in the corner of her balcony. Her eyes burned all that day, and everyone who saw Azra in the village asked why her eyes were so red.

"If you swim that much with your eyes open underwater, you'll change into a fish," Fatima teased her. Whereas her eyes were also just as red. "Let's go there again. We've learned the way anyway," she added. "Maybe I'll take a starfish for myself too."

After that day, from time to time, Azra found a fish on her door ready for cooking: a dentex, a small tuna, or a grouper. She recognized them by the spear's hole. She smiled, for he had found the money to buy a new one.

Azra hadn't heard from the swimmer in years.

REMEMBERING THAT SHE STILL HAD the starfish made Azra smile. "It's been years since that day," she murmured. Fatima's laughter echoed through the deserted cove before the memory of her friend vanished like the fog that had enveloped the shore. Now alone on the empty beach, Azra reckoned that seventeen months had passed since Aegean had receded from the coast. Sitting on the derelict boat had gotten her dress muddy, but Azra was unconcerned. It was time to see the Pearl Seller again. She didn't want to be late. The pebbles crunched where Azra landed as she jumped off. She brushed the dirt on her green dress with her hands, but it didn't really work.

This would be their third meeting. The absent sea had drawn them closer to each other. They both wanted to bring her back. After the forest fire, Azra almost lost hope. However, like a firefly, she had a little light that shone within. Without hesitation, she walked up to the marble wall and passed it as soon as possible. In their last meeting, he had promised to tell a story about the black seaweed that was common along their village. Deep in thoughts, Azra arrived at his house.

Before knocking on the door, she took a deep breath and whispered, "I want to know the Pearl Seller's real name. I won't leave the house without asking him. Have some courage, Azra. Nothing will go wrong."

The old man opened the door instantly and said, "You are just on time. I was waiting for you." When they met a couple of days ago, he had been more anxious. But now, he looked rested, as if his worries had left him for a while. He hoped talking with Azra and sharing their fears about the village would calm him further.

When Azra entered the house, she noticed the white, translucent lace curtains that hung over the windows which looked out to the sea. She didn't like them. A year ago, they weren't there. It was almost impossible to see through them. They made the room seem smaller and more stuffy. The old man went into the kitchen, preparing food for his guest. She could hear the Pearl Seller working without seeing him.

Of course, he didn't listen to Azra when she said, "Please don't make anything for me. I want to listen to your story. Let's sit."

"You come to my house, and I don't offer you anything? Ha, it can't happen! You know, it's not only for my pearls but also for my coffee people visit over and over again. If you keep insisting on not trying it, you will regret it your whole life. So, tell me, do you like your coffee with sugar or plain?"

Azra smiled and said, "Plain, please. No sugar, no milk."

The kitchen door was in front of her. She could not see inside but could follow the man's shadow as it moved along the ground through the crack at the bottom of the door. She could hear his deep breathing, cautious footsteps, and the dings and clatter from whatever his nervous hands were manipulating. She listened to the boiling water, the sound of plates clanging, and a knife on a cutting board slicing something, probably fruit. One of the slices must have fallen since the Pearl Seller picked something up and washed it well. Then, he turned off the water. Neither he nor Azra was in a hurry. They could have spent eternity in this slow ritual, reluctant to start discussing what they feared was waiting for them in the future. They needed time to find solutions, and being slow helped them to think clearly.

She was thinking, "Will he tell me everything he knew? How will I ask him his name?" But didn't dare to say it aloud.

The old man opened the cupboard again and grabbed two cups while the coffee was boiling. The smell of coffee spread throughout the house. It reminded Azra of Eid mornings, a day of celebration. The last fun one seemed like millennia ago. Throughout that day, her family had visited all their neighbors in the village, practically everyone, and had some sweets and coffee. When she was a little girl, she recalled waiting for the hosts to bring candy, coffee, and sometimes gifts for the kids. Everyone was in the village then. None of them had left yet.

Her eyes returned to the curtains. Handmade, old fashioned curtains next to white walls. She decided to get up and open them. But just as she rose, the old man came in with a tray. On it were cookies and apples with the coffee. The design of the cups caught her attention. They were larger than usual and featured a basket pattern of strawberries and cherries on the exterior.

"This is much better. Now we can sit," the Pearl Seller said.

Azra gestured to the curtains with her hand, "Can I open them? They weren't here on my last visit."

"A lot has changed since your last visit, Azra. You know that. A year ago, we thought the sound of the waves would never leave. But if you want to open them, feel free."

The young woman got up, opened them, and saw an astonishing landscape. The ocean's shoreline and waves had receded and been replaced by a desert. Although she already knew that, seeing it at the Pearl Seller's house was still startling as if everything would be different here. Aegean was faintly visible near the horizon. To the left, traces of the fire were evident; the scorched branches of the ash forest stretched forlornly toward the sky. Azra shuddered, feeling guilty for imagining a different view. She sat down abruptly, the curtains wide open. The old man shrugged and stated, "The white curtains are better to look at than the abandoned shore. Seeing all that brown sand makes me lose hope. I don't want to live in a desert! My wife,

Melike, made them when I was far away from home once. She used to crochet when she wasn't staring at the waves, waiting for me to return. I ignored what she did—the waiting, the chasing after the children. When she finished embroidering the curtains, she showed them to me. I'm ashamed when I recall my reaction. I wish..." he paused, then raised his voice in an angrier tone, "'Put these rags away. Don't you dare cover the view with them!' That's what I said. Melike remained silent and seemed to listen. Years passed, and her death taught me a lesson I will never forget. Around that time, I began to withdraw from the sea, and now, unexpectedly, the sea has withdrawn from us. I can't get used to looking at this ominous desert. I am drowning in the remnants of what Melike left behind."

He straightened up, squared his shoulders, and put his cup on the table, "There is only one thing I want to do: bring Aegean back. At any cost, I must see the waves crash on our shores again."

The Pearl Seller turned his face toward the abandoned shore. Azra could not see his gaze, but she was sure his eyes were filled with tears. The old man was trying to escape from the depths of his memories and return to the present. He sipped his coffee and cleared his throat with a cough. Azra was afraid to breathe. She didn't move, thinking that if she said anything, the Pearl Seller would start crying. Silently, she looked out into the void where the waves once danced. Before meeting the Pearl Seller, she imagined him as a hero. He was the only person in the village who had to sail out to the farthest shores. The old man had collected many pearls on his travels and started selling them. But now, what she saw in front of her was a human trying to not cry. It was as if he had given up on being a hero years ago.

Afraid of making noise, Azra held her cup carefully, and as soon as she tasted it, she said, "This is wondrous! I've never tasted something like it before!"

The Pearl Seller became enthusiastic. He turned to Azra again, smiled, and said, "I told you so! I brought the beans from a distant place, from the lands to the south, where the climate is hot and humid and the soil is rich. The beans are harvested by hand and roasted in a special way. It has a rich, earthy flavor that is truly distinctive. But unfortunately, I don't have much left. From time to time, I used to travel there. However, I don't know how many years have passed since my last visit."

Azra took another sip. This coffee was different than what she had expected. The taste was lighter, and the cup was much larger than what she was used to. She drank it quickly. When there was only a little left, she touched the bottom of the hot cup with her index finger, dipping it into what was left of the thick brew. There were no coffee grains at the bottom, and her finger burned. She swiftly put it in her mouth and sucked it to reduce the pain.

"This is really light, and there are no grains at the bottom!" she said, "do you have a special name for it?"

"Well, it's just coffee, no other name," the Pearl Seller smiled.

"Why didn't you offer me this coffee last year when I first visited you?" She paused, and for a second, she thought maybe she shouldn't have said it, but it was too late. "I remember the hibiscus tea burnt my tongue that day, and now I've burnt my finger." They both laughed.

The old man shrugged, "That day, it was time to have some hibiscus tea; today, it's time for coffee. Life never gives you what you expect. Do you want another cup?"

Azra nodded eagerly and answered, "Yes!" She hadn't expected the coffee to be so good. While waiting, she stood up and slowly opened the cupboard doors in the corner. Azra didn't want to make any sound and anxiously turned to look back toward the kitchen just to check. The old man was still preparing the coffee. Hurriedly she looked inside and found a notebook, some pens, and a locked box. The pages of the notebook were old and yellowish. The Pearl Seller's handwriting was like a storm, impossible to read. In blue ink, he had written, *"Today ... of my departure from ..."* The sounds coming from the kitchen had stopped. The old man was standing right behind Azra. She couldn't look into his eyes. They both were silent. Azra's face was red with embarrassment.

Without saying anything, the Pearl Seller offered the second coffee to her, closed the cabinet's doors, and said, "Well. Where were we?" He was trying to sound cheerful, but there was a hint of disappointment in his voice.

Without looking at him, Azra said, "I am sorry." She was still looking at the ground.

"Oh, don't worry," the old man said, "Perhaps one day I'll tell you the story of the notebook and the locked box. But not today. Oh well... curiosity can be a good sign. I was inquisitive and naughty when I was young, and I don't regret it. However, nobody likes someone sneaking through their personal items. Next time ask. It would be nicer, but don't expect me to say 'yes,' every time. Now, there is so much to tell. Today, I'm perplexed. My mind is like a secret library that hasn't been opened for a long time. Messy, dusty, and crowded."

The young woman looked at the man's disheveled white hair with parts sticking out into the air. She wanted to catch some of his memories. But she chose not to say anything and sipped her coffee.

He stood up, slapping his hands on his knees, "I'm so dull today. I'm not always like this, so don't get too worried. If you have finished your cup, let's go out on the balcony and get some fresh air. I need a change."

"Follow me," he said, marching purposefully down the narrow hallway. The walls on either side were adorned with an eclectic mix of paintings, sculptures, and trinkets, giving the space the feel of a grand collector's chamber. Unfortunately, Azra didn't have enough time to examine them. One was a work of colorful fingerprints of a child, and another she passed quickly by was some intricate cross-stitch patterns that must have taken months to embroider. It was obvious that they were a woman's belongings. The skeletal remains of various strange fish were also hanging here and there. The hallway seemed to stretch on endlessly without indicating where it might lead. Its dark yellow walls only added to her sense of disorientation.

The Pearl Seller turned into a room on his left. Azra stopped walking and looked around for a little before entering. While the hallway was long, she noticed a few other rooms, but the doors were all closed. Finally, Azra entered the room in amazement: The room was full of various pieces of intricate jewelry. Her eyes were dazed. For a moment, Azra forgot about the disasters that had befallen her and her village and approached one of the display cases, drawn in by the beauty of its jewels on display.

"These are lovely," she said, gesturing towards the pearls.

The old man was proud of his work. "Thank you. Is there something in particular that catches your eye?"

Azra's gaze fell on a necklace with a large, luminous pearl at its center. "That one is beautiful. Is it for sale?"

The Pearl Seller named a price that made Azra's eyebrows shoot up. "That's quite expensive," she said.

"Ah, but worth every kuruş," he replied. "These pearls are the finest in the lands. They are harvested from oysters that dwell only in the deepest, purest waters."

"I see. Probably I'll never have one." Azra said with admiration.

"You should know that not everyone is allowed in this room. So please don't tell anyone about what you've seen here," said the man while going out onto the room's balcony.

On the balcony, Azra was greeted with a view of a beautiful garden. After the outlandish curtains and bewitching jewels, the sight of the bushes and trees was refreshing.

“The sea has left us, but not the snow or rain. The streams from the mountains keep the soil fertile,” the man said. “Fortunately, we still have these blessings for which we are thankful. I’ve also learned to protect this garden with glass walls, which I open when the weather warms up.”

“The fact that it’s away from fires has also protected it. Otherwise, this garden would have been destroyed,” Azra stated. She hesitated briefly before changing the subject, sweeping her eyes over the olive trees, roses, and countless flowers. The scent of the plants was pleasant and calming. “One must forget all their troubles here,” she remarked, leaning against the balcony’s railing as if for support.

“You should see it in the spring,” the Pearl Seller replied.

“Well, I’ve learned much about you today. But I still need to know your name. I’m tired of calling you “the Pearl Seller.”

“Oh, I should have let you know before. I don’t like that title, either. I’ve had a variety of names and titles in different places. Before I started to dive and collect pearls from the depths of the sea, they called me “The Captain.” In some places, people call me “The Merchant.” Nevertheless, after so long at sea and so many voyages, I was a different man when I returned to settle down here. Part of me wanted to get away from crowded places. I was tired of curious eyes and ridiculous questions. When they couldn’t get answers from me, they started spreading rumors. Some parts were true, and many were lies. People began whispering, and calling me ‘The Pearl Seller,’ which at first didn’t annoy me. It was good for trade. However, my father named me Fahad after his own father. It was my grandfather who had come to this village from the Eastern side of the world.”

“Yes, Fahad is not a common name in this area. I wonder how your grandfather found this place. The feet of many are unfamiliar with these lands. We love to stay hidden behind the brushes, as you know.”

"Some people also like to find hidden things," he stroked his darkened beard. "It's in my family's blood. But my grandma was from the town's mountainside," said the Pearl Seller.

They stared at the bare branches of the trees. It was a winter balcony with a glass enclosure to protect from the cold. There were some saplings but Azra didn't know what kind of trees they would become. They were silent for a while. The birds were chirping even though it was winter.

Then, he began...

"A sunken ship with a dead crew. My story started from nothing. I was a prisoner on a monk's island. After almost starving to death in their dungeon for who knows how many days, the abbot set me free. But it was a strange freedom. It was good to no longer be in chains or locked in a cell, and I was happy to be outside. However, there was nowhere to go on the island except the monastery and a few small buildings belonging to the monks, with few narrow roads leading between them. So, on the first day of my freedom, I searched the whole isle but found nothing other than those silent monks. I was not one of them, and they kept their secrets to themselves, trying to hide everything from me. The monks let me to live, and it was enough for me. I felt lucky to breath. Some days, I sat on the ground and watched them. The monks had a strict hierarchy. Some were busy gathering wood, and some worked with iron. There were cooks and gardeners. There were librarians responsible for their scrolls and books, and there were clerks and even some who painted.

"To pass the time, I became an apprentice under one who was a carpenter with a shop of his own. I can still remember his blue eyes under his loose brown hood. I'd always dreamed of building a ship, but the task felt impossible. My master never made any promises. Being busy allowed my mind to heal. We repaired old furniture and built new shelves and tables. He never asked me to return each day, but he seemed relaxed about having someone to help.

"One day, while shaping a wood block, I made a mistake, breaking it into two and cutting a deep wound on my right hand. The broken pieces were instantly coated in red. I seized my hand with the other and screamed. My master took my injured hand, set a large green leaf on top of it, and then tightened it with a white cloth.

"He curtly rebuked me. 'Too much noise for a small cut.'

"It had been the first time somebody had spoken to me in many days. That instant, I forgot the pain and realized how much I missed talking with someone. I couldn't say a word.

"He continued, 'Go rest. Come back tomorrow. I'll look at your hand again.'

"I can remember his soft voice. And I briefly considered if it was worth hurting myself again so that somebody else would break their silence and speak with me.

"I stepped outside the shop again, but the familiar sight of the narrow roads on the island brought back unpleasant memories of my early days there. The looming walls of the monastery appeared hostile and unforgiving. As I made my way along the quiet paths, I could hear faint whispers and the sound of footsteps echoing in the distance. Now with nothing to occupy my time, I decided to explore further. Peeking into the kitchen, the tantalizing aroma of soup and the smell of fresh bread wafting through the air reminded me of my hunger, but I didn't want to disturb the busy cooks.

"I continued on in silence until I came upon the library. I wasn't a great reader, but 'This was before you lost your ship and crew,' I reminded myself. 'You left your home. No one wants to talk. So why are you hesitating going into a library?' With that thought, I found myself standing inside the shadowy building.

"An old monk with piercing, cold black eyes greeted me, the rest of his face partially concealed by his hood. I awkwardly said 'Hello,' unsure of what else to say in this silent world. 'Hello! Hello! Hello!' my voice echoed back from the corners of the cold stones.

"Instead of answering, the monk trembled with rage. His thick woolen robe could not hide his fury.

"I took a deep breath and headed towards the reading room, with the old monk following closely behind. I sat at an empty desk and witnessed the monk disappear. A while later, he returned with a piece of paper, and placing it in front of me, he vanished once again.

"The paper read, 'Welcome! I understand that you do not know that a foreigner who washes up half-dead on the island's shore is not to be greeted aloud by the Olikan cult. It has been a long time since our library was visited by uninvited eyes. You are the first visitor we have allowed to enter in many, many years –with the abbot's permission, of course. You may read as you wish, but remember our rules: Do not touch the books in the leftmost chamber, and do not enter the room at the front of the library. Our rules are simple, and there's no reason why they shouldn't be followed. First and foremost, you must obey the law of silence that our Great Creator expects of us. Yours sincerely, Anthon.'

"'Anthon,' I whispered to myself, grateful for the chance to communicate with someone on this lonely island. "The Law of Silence" seemed like a death sentence. I browsed the shelves of books while my wounded hand throbbed in pain. The dressing the carpenter had wrapped around it was stained with blood. Ignoring the pain, I casually pulled a book from the shelves. As I flipped through the pages, I memorized the miniatures and the familiar words I encountered. It distracted my mind to have something other to think about than the pain. I decided to spend as much time as possible in this temple of books. Unfortunately, it took a long time for the wound to heal.

"The next day, early morning, I went to the carpenter's shop to have my wound re-wrapped. My master preferred to remain silent. Whenever I was tempted to speak, I remembered the law. The wound still stung, but the clean dressing relieved my hand. I hurried back to the library. Anthon's dark eyes flickered from under his hood. I nodded and headed for the reading room. I wasn't in a hurry and had lots of time to spend. I found books about other distant seas, of finding pearls, and diaries by those who have traveled far. Some of them were too long or written in different languages. However, it wasn't hard for me to find books in my native tongue. Finding the interesting ones and reading them took several weeks.

"At night, I read by candlelight. Sometimes, I nodded off, and when I opened my eyes, the candle was long cold. The darkness all around frightened me. In Anthon's place, a new monk, also hidden under a hood, came to stand guard. The night watchman seemed to prefer leaving me be. His inexperienced hands suggested he was younger than Anthon. I couldn't take books out of the library, so Anthon showed me a small stall where I could study and silently handed me a piece of paper that read: 'You can sleep here.'

"Being separate from the monks and not sharing their responsibilities made life easy. However, one night at dinner, a note was quietly slipped next to my plate: 'Until when?' It wasn't in Anthon's handwriting. It was written in yellow, insidious ink. What did it mean? I couldn't tell if it was a threat or a warning. Perhaps one of the monks had written the note just to unsettle me."

"My wound had healed, and the note was a reminder that I should get back to the carpenter and my wish to build a ship. I returned to help the carpenter for a few days. But a voice inside me, one that I couldn't silence, lured me back to the library, telling me I wasn't ready for shipbuilding yet. I followed my inner voice and withdrew from the carpenter's shop. I returned to the library and my stall, surrounding myself with a wall of thick books to shut out the monks. I had almost gotten used to ignoring their presence and, sometimes, talking to myself, not communicating with any of them. That is until I found a new note among the pages I was reading:

"'May the forgiving mercy of the holy book Olikan be upon you, and may the wrath of our abbot Frederik stay forever far away. Place the tenth book from the second shelf from the bottom in the leftmost room, on the table by the right window, and always feel our invisible helping hand on your shoulder. You don't want that helping hand to become the blind hand of an executioner.'

"I was being asked to break the rules of the library. My eyes searched for Anthon. He seemed busy with some obscure business under his hood. I turned to the table by the right window, where someone was sitting, also hidden under a brown robe. His back was turned to me, but he wore a unique ring on his pinky finger. The shining sapphire stone stirred my fears. I did not know what the penalties for breaking the rules would be, but the note threatened death. I thought of my tiny room, the books waiting to be read, and the two meals I was graciously given morning and night. I remembered the day I woke up in the dungeon, the abbot's words, and then, as if nothing had happened, I found myself back in the refectory."

"A note was flung onto the plate before me: 'Until when?'

"One of the monks dropped a bowl of wine on the floor. The red wine seeped through the shards to my feet. That evening, I was the first to leave the refectory. The next day, I picked up the book from the left chamber and, with trembling hands, placed it on the table by the right window. The monk with the sapphire ring, sitting at the table the day before, looked up from under his hood as if to thank me, greeting me with his eyes, and for a long time, did not bother me. My heart was racing. Whenever I saw Anthon, my hands shook, and I feared he would place an angry note in front of me. However, the silence in the sanctuary of books was not broken. The leftmost room and the forbidden books, Anthon's silence, the threats I received, and the unbreakable stillness on the island... Why not? A wolf was in my gut, circling in my mind, prodding at my fears, urging me to explore the forbidden shelves."

"In that area, I came across the book on the legends of the Simurgh. I was fascinated by the description of the feathers and their myriad of miraculous properties. But I doubted its authenticity. The feathers are not in plain sight. They are very rare and often offered as prized secret gifts. And reaching the mountain of Qaf is no easy feat. Various paths had been tried and failed. But if we truly have one, your feather, we must learn how to use it to our advantage."

Azra was engrossed in Fahad's tale, but a particular detail caught her attention. "Wait, did you say you ventured into the forbidden chamber? How did you summon the courage?"

"Patience," said the Pearl Seller. "I pushed my luck and continued to browse the shelves in the left chamber. Anthon's unresponsiveness lulled me into complacency and eased my fears. I found another book there, Azra. This one was about black mosses containing more practical methods than finding the Simurgh. Be careful, Azra. I am not talking about just any moss. This rare and unique plant grows only along the recesses of the Mossy Village. In the book, it was referred to as Neptune's thread. There were long descriptions of various poisons and inconceivable spells. I was excited—if I went back home, I could try out all I had read about on my own. I just needed the seaweed from our shores. I wrote down what I had learned and looked for other books to better decipher the complex language of the book. My dream of building a boat was rekindled, and I began thinking about how to leave the island.

"As the days passed, I discovered the island's secrets, the strict hierarchy of the Olikan sect, and the roles of the monks in the monastery.

Of course, I can't explain it all, but the key figure for me was Anthon. He was a close friend of the abbot. After entrusting the library to his apprentice, he would go to the abbot's room. Sometimes, he came back with sealed letters. I understood that they preferred not to speak to each other either. I was not the only one they communicated with by writing. It was part of their religious beliefs to remain silent except on rare occasions. Those who kept their silence were elevated in rank, their dignity multiplied. It was their custom to burn sealed letters after reading them so as not to reveal their secrets. The monks seemed to have no contact with the outside world. However, twice a week, a loaded ship arrived on the island, bringing news, tools, and food from their royal patron, to which they were bound. This ship carried young novices and took traveling monks back to the city.

"I was determined to unravel the mysteries of Neptune's thread and had come across dozens of books about the black moss. I couldn't leave the island yet. One evening, as I fell asleep amongst the books, I was awakened by the sound of a bell in the distance. I had never heard bells on the island before. Why had they chosen this evening? Was it an alarm or a call for a meeting? I had no idea. I rushed to the window to see where the sound was coming from. The winding roads of the island were empty. I wanted to run to the front room to see if there was any movement, but Anthon's old figure stood before me, his silent eyes fixed on me.

"Succumbing to an old habit, I asked, 'Did you hear the bell?'

"Anthon's stony lips reminded me of the books I had taken from the left stall without permission. I couldn't go any further or push the limits anymore. When I returned to my desk, the books I had read were gone. A warning was written on the notes I had taken: 'You have broken the law of silence and touched books that a stranger should not touch. If you ignore our rules again, the library doors will be closed to you forever. Fear what will happen to you.'

“I had inevitably learned the laws of the Olikan sect, but I did not know what punishments they imposed. Although this uncertainty frightened me, I was relieved that my notes were still there. I had to unravel the secrets of Neptune’s thread. Restraining my curiosity, I refrained from entering the left chamber until another menacing command found me: ‘The forgiving compassion of the holy book Olikan is helping you. You owe your readings on Neptune’s thread to that compassion. I hid your notes from Anthon, or he would have taken them and burned them to ashes in the fire of his rage. And you would have gotten your share of the flames. If you wish to continue your research, you must return to the left side before you incur the wrath of Abbot Frederik. Leave the fourth book from the left on the top shelf on my desk so that your peaceful reading is not interrupted. Otherwise, I will not be responsible for what happens to you.’

“It was an anonymous note, but clearly from the sapphire-ringed monk. I noticed that he hadn’t written his name. He knew how to protect himself. At first, I thought of showing the note to Anthon, but the librarian’s warnings prevented me from trusting him. I was caught between two groups of monks: the authority of the monastery and those of heresy. One way or another, I was bound to upset someone and end up in a bad way. Yet, I didn’t want to leave the island until I knew the mystery of the black moss.”

“The threatening letters I had received and the burning itch of curiosity demanded action. I waited for nightfall. The night watchman took Anthon’s place when I was ready to leave for the night. Silently, I took the requested book from the forbidden chamber and placed it on the sapphire-ringed monk’s desk. With my confidence renewed, I was no longer as frightened and worried but had the coolness of a seasoned thief. The next night, I pulled another book, one that would be useful to me, from the forbidden shelves: *Recipes from Neptune’s Thread.*

"It was in those pages that I came across Lilith. The book about the mysteries of moss featured a witch named Lilith and her discoveries. The recipes were her creations. A chapter titled 'Lilith's Castle' described where the witch lived and how to find her. It was not far from the island where I was. The last chapter included maps showing how to reach her.

"Suddenly, my plan changed. Now I knew where I was going. Among those pages, I came across a sketched portrait of Lilith, a beauty like no other. Her innocent face, framed by wavy hair, whispered that I had to see her immediately. Among the potions she prepared with Neptune's thread were concoctions that could ease my travels. In the stories I had read, it was rumored that she had discovered the elixir of immortality.

Two centuries ago, Solomon, the ruler of the eastern regions, had imprisoned Lilith deep underground. But somehow, years later, she had emerged from the underworld and taken up residence in an abandoned castle. She was a witch known for casting dark spells. Yet, her innocent face suggested otherwise. I couldn't decide until I met her. I needed Lilith's help to solve the mysteries of Neptune's thread.

"The bell rang twice. This time, it was deafening. The shrill sound lingered in my ears for a long time. Anthon's angry eyes flashed before me. For the first time, I saw his face wrinkled with rage, his lips tight with hatred. The last thing I remembered before everything went black was his vengeful gaze. When I awoke, I found myself in the dungeon. If Milas, the sapphire-ringed monk whose name I later learned, hadn't kept his word and abandoned me, I would have worn those chains until the end of my days. A note passed through the taverns and inns that night, and the iron gate was thrown wide open. As the night shrouded the island's streets in darkness, I secretly boarded the ship led by Milas. As the boat set sail in the harbor, I feared that I would be caught and that, this time, there would be no escaping death. But thankfully, I was wrong."

"As the ship left the island and sailed towards the city, Milas, the man who had brought these misfortunes upon me, removed his hood and said, 'The Law of Silence is behind us.' His voice was sharper than I expected. His face, previously hidden, was somber. 'I am writing a book on the law's irrelevance in the Olikan sect, and the king supports the idea. Without his support, neither you nor I would have escaped alive.'

"I couldn't take my eyes off the Island of the Monks, fading into the distance, appearing and disappearing between the waves as it sank beneath the horizon. I was saved, though I still have nightmares of that ordeal that haunted my sleep. Regardless, being smuggled out of the monastery allowed my journey to Lilith.

"When I finally set foot on land, Milas handed me the notes I had taken on the island and gave me the book *The Thread of Neptune* from his leather bag. Among his gifts was a new book, *Posidonia Oceanica*. He bid me farewell, saying, 'I thought this book would be useful for you as well, regarding what you've read and the notes you took. Consider it a memento of our little collaboration.' Milas and I never crossed paths again."

The Pearl Seller paused. He took a deep breath as he touched the scar on his arm. Azra stood up and opened one of the windows. The cool air entering the garden brought some relief. She thought of Lilith, whom Sevim had mentioned in her notes, and what the black moss had brought her.

"It's already dark," Fahad said, "that's enough for now. You should think about what I've told you, Azra. What I mean is that you should go to Lilith, too. Find her. Go to Lilith's castle."

"Never," Azra revealed, "I've never left this town. How am I to do this?"

The dark waves stirred in the Pearl Seller's blue eyes. Fahad seemed to be hiding the sea within. He said, "If you want the sea to return to our village, you must journey there and seek her wisdom. Otherwise, our village, I'm afraid, is lost. My story is over, and now yours must begin."

The garden was pitch black. A freezing cold accompanied the darkness. There were few stars in the sky. Yet the pearls, forgotten back in the room, shone faintly like pale fireflies. Fahad insisted Azra stay overnight, it was dangerous to walk in the forest at night. But she needed to go home and be alone for a while. The black moss reminded her of someone she didn't want to think about. When she got home, she quickly climbed the wooden stairs and went straight to bed, wrapping herself tightly in a blanket. She cried. Perhaps all night.

CHAPTER FIVE

The Breath Thief

Kamasis

AZRA ARRIVED IN KAMASIS, KNOWING exactly where to go this time. Fahad had given her directions, telling her to walk past the town square and up the Kandil slope. The slope curved up to the right and led to a vast plain. There, behind the pine trees, she would find a two-story wooden house.

"Just say, 'I bring Fahad's greetings,'" the Pearl Seller had told her. "I can't accompany you, but I'm giving you a key to open the doors you'll knock on. My greeting will protect you like the angel on your right shoulder."

She did as he instructed. A stocky man with a black mustache opened the door, looked at Azra with half-sleepy, half-condescending eyes, and asked, "Who are you looking for?" Hearing the name of the Pearl Seller enlivened him, and at once, he jumped in front of the young woman and started shouting, "Fahriye!"

"What is it?" A woman wearing slippers and holding a towel in her hand came down from upstairs, looking weary and annoyed.

"Mr. Fahad, the master pearl seller, has sent us a guest. I am heading down to the bazaar. I have some business there." Then he turned to Azra and said, "My wife will take care of you."

As Azra climbed the wooden stairs to the room Fahriye showed her, she felt a twinge of estrangement, for the first time in her life she was among strangers.

Fahriye pointed to the bed and said, "You can sleep here." She opened the doors of the wall closets in the room and hurriedly emptied the drawers inside. As she was taking away the items, she gestured towards Azra's suitcase with her eyes and said, "You can put your things there in the closet." She quickly returned with some towels and placed them on the bed, stating, "These are clean. Use them as you like." Next, Fahriye straightened out the bed sheets with her hands, adding, "The sheets are like new. Rest assured, no one has used them. Mr. Fahad sleeps here when he visits us, yet these visits rarely happen." At last, she nodded and left, closing the door behind her with an uneasy smile, "Rest, my dear, you must be tired."

Azra sat on the bed and remained still for a while. She had packed up and left her village days ago. And for the first time since, she breathed a sigh of relief. Azra still had her coat on. When she opened the window, a bit uneasy about what she might find, the noise of the city poured in unbidden. The town square peeked through the pine trees at the bottom of the slope. Azra would only stay here for three days on her journey to Lilith's castle. After Kamasis, she would stop in Narlı, then continue to Glass Island, where she would take a boat to the witch's island. According to Fahad's estimations, the voyage should take about two weeks. The Pearl Seller had calculated every step Azra would need to take. He had identified the people to meet, writing down their names, who she would talk to, what to discuss, and where she would find what was needed. Unless, of course, something went wrong and ruin his carefully laid plans.

She took off her coat and hung it up. Then Azra unpacked a few items from her suitcase, placing them in the closet Fahriye had shown her. Next, she skimmed through the Pearl Seller's notes, making a mental list of what she needed to do and the shops she needed to visit while in Kamasis. And then the young traveler recalled how she had been convinced to leave the Mossy Village.

THE MORNING AFTER HEARING FAHAD'S story, sleep finally came to Azra, only to be awakened by a powerful dream that sent shivers through her. The sun was shining high in the sky, and the broad leaves of her fig tree and the flowers blooming in the garden reminded her of summer. While having breakfast on the balcony as usual, all of a sudden, Azrafelt something strange under her feet. The balcony's marble floor was covered in water. Looking up, the fig tree's leaves were drenched, with water dripping from them as though it had just rained, yet the sky was clear with no clouds. When she went into the garden to investigate, she noticed waves of water lapping against the fence. Aegean could not have come so far inland; it knew where to stop, yet still, the sea overflowed. Azra's feet started to sink into the muddy soil. As the water reached her waist, she tried to move her but couldn't free herself from being pulled down. The earth, like quicksand, started dragging her deeper and deeper. She shouted in panic, but it was no use. There was no one around—only the scorching sun.

Azra woke up sweating and shivering. Soon after, there was a knock at the door. She hadn't yet recovered from the dream but went downstairs without delay. Azra opened the door and found Fahad standing there, clearly having been through a rough night as well.

"I was worried about you. You ran away last night. Are you okay?" Fahad asked.

Azra looked down at her feet. There was neither mud nor water. "I'm fine," she replied simply.

The old man's worry was evident on his face. He was holding a heavy leather bag, obviously not yet finished with what he had started. What Fahad had said last night had shaken Azra to her core, but she couldn't be angry with him for it. She invited the old man in, immediately started brewing some tea, and took out some of the dried figs she had prepared during the summer. "I don't have flavored coffees, but I do have fresh tea. Delicious!" she announced.

"I'm sorry, I was a bit too hard on you last night," Fahad said as he tried one of the dried figs and sipped his tea.

"No, you were right," Azra responded, tugging at the sleeves of her sweater. She was angry with herself for so quickly agreeing with Fahad. Her eyes were contemplative, yet under her disheveled hair, a sharp determination was visible on her pale face. The last few days' events were compelling her to do something. Azra had to act. Lifting her gaze from the floor, she spoke firmly, "I was the one who was dying to hear your story. Now, I have to bear the consequences. I can't live with myself, hiding in nightmares and memories. I must go. I must find Lilith.'"

THE DOOR OF THE ROOM opened slowly. Fahriye poked her head through the crack and said, "I was going to tell you that dinner is ready. I didn't want to disturb you."

"I'll be right there," Azra replied, shaking off her thoughts.

Dinner was served under Fahriye's watchful eyes and accompanied by Rashid's loud chewing. Rashidhad returned from the bazaar with bags of groceries, and the smell of oranges permeated the house as soon as he arrived. Because they had company, his wife had prepared meat, potatoes, and salad. Seeing the table, Azra realized her hunger and ate two plates of everything. Fahriye and Rashid, a middle-aged, childless couple, lived in their unique way. Rashid was Fahad's right-hand man, the only one who found him customers, who would act as an intermediary, and traveled to different cities to sell when necessary. He was Fahad's link to the outside world.

The sole topic of conversation at dinner was the receding sea. Kamasis had been affected by the absence of Aegean, but its connections to other cities and trade networks had sustained its people. They had no news of the fire that had broken out near the Mossy Village.

"How could we know?" Rashid exclaimed. "Mr. Fahad lives as an enigma, one he doesn't want solved. I only see him when he comes to town."

Azra put her fork down and slowly swallowed the last bite in her mouth. As she took a sip of water from her glass, Fahriye passed a plate of sliced oranges in front of her.

"Maybe later," Azra said. "I suddenly showed up at your door, and you opened your home to me, giving me a place at your table."

"Of course," Fahriye smiled, placing her hand on the young woman's shoulder. "Mr. Fahad trusts us and sends a rare person like you to our door." Rashid nodded as he chewed. The husband and wife's eyes were locked on the young woman.

"With your permission, I will stay for two more days. I am a stranger in Kamasis. I need to see *Sahaf* Halil Efendi, the collector of second-hand books. I also need to prepare for the rest of my journey."

"Sahaf Halil Efendi," Rashid murmured. The man had recently closed his shop. I haven't met him personally, but I've heard his name often. Tomorrow, we'll go down to the bazaar and ask around."

"I'll come too," Fahriye stated, standing up to collect the empty plates. Azra also got up to help her. Rashid took another slice of orange.

THE CITY HAD NOT YET awakened. The Kandil slope was shrouded in white fog, and the condensation escaping from the mouths of the trio descending the slope mixed with it. Fahriye clung to Azra's arm while Rashid walked with a comfortable gait. As he surveyed the fog, he stated, "It will lift in an hour and slowly dissipate," adding, "Let's wander a bit until the city awakens. Don't depart without witnessing the beauty of Kamasis."

"For God's sake, there's no beauty left!" Fahriye snapped, gripping Azra's arm tightly.

"It's just a figure of speech, woman; don't nitpick," Rashid replied, his speech unbroken by her outburst. "What else could I say?"

Fahriye glared at her husband, then rolled her eyes and shifted her gaze to Azra. "Since the sea receded, we've lost our essence," she grieved, "Despair has spread like a disease among both those who left and those who remain. You won't find the old cheerfulness or bustle on these streets. That house over there thrived on fishing. Captain Reza's children used to sell fruit even in the summers. And now? The captain has secluded himself at home while his children have moved away." She gestured towards Captain Reza's house and pointed to the windows. "Look, I'll be damned if he isn't spying on us from behind those drawn curtains. I can't begin to tell you how listless he's become. The great Captain Reza can't even step outside. And his wife was unbearable. I don't know how anyone could live in that house with her."

"Fahriye," Rashid elongated the last syllable of her name, this time placing his hands in his pockets. "Don't upset her. She's traveled a long way and still has further to go. Let's not add more to her burden."

"I'm fine," Azra assured, lifting her shoulders slightly, "Captain Reza's situation feels all too familiar. Our village is almost in ruins. It's all but abandoned, and now goblins play there." Her shoulders sagged involuntarily. Azra lowered her gaze towards the road, her expression grim. She raised her coat collar a bit higher and tried to warm her hands with her breath.

The fog gradually lifted over the city. If only it could have remained, concealing the despair. The absence of Aegean had transformed Kamasis into a soulless husk. Azra felt a burning in her heart as she walked towards the town square. The bench where she and Elmados had previously said goodbye stood empty. There was no market; no stalls were set up. Most of the townspeople had yet to arrive, still clinging to their sleepiness. The last day she had seen the ghost flashed before her eyes. She gripped Fahriye's arm as though seeking strength. She wondered where Elmados was now. The boats in the harbor lay stuck in the sand, some tilted sideways, others overturned.

Rashid jumped onto one of them and declared, "This was our ship," noting, "It's been scrapped. Half of my work has vanished."

Fahriye and Azra also boarded the ship and climbed up to the wheelhouse. The barren landscape in front of them silenced them all, and they ceased talking. Rattles emanated from wooden gaps—likely, the ship was infested with rats. They returned to the old shoreline in silence.

"Actually, I need a ship and a captain, but I can't use yours. Fahad estimates the sea is about a day's sail from Kamasis. How far has Aegean retreated? After I leave you, I must cross the Ida Mountains and reach Narlı."

"Mr. Fahad is correct in his estimate," Rashid confirmed. "If we leave without delay, we are a day's sail away. Unfortunately, my ship is now useless. Anyway, let's find Sahaf Halil. First, let's head to the tea shop. Shopkeepers don't open their shops without their morning tea. People gather there early."

At the tea shop, they found a few shopkeepers stirring their tea with sleepy eyes, each seated at separate tables, appearing as if they had sleepwalked in. All, including the boy who served the tea, had streaks of gray in their hair, particularly noticeable along their brows. Azra found this odd but said nothing. She and Fahriye sat at a table together, and without asking, the boy placed two teacups in front of them. The steam from the tea warmed Azra's face. Rashid, meanwhile, visited the other tables, speaking in whispers. He then returned and sat down with them.

"Sahaf Halil hasn't been seen much since he closed his shop," Rashid informed them. Pointing to a man at one of the tables, he continued, "He told me where the Sahaf lives. Finish your teas, and let's go check on him."

Azra knocked three times, Fahad's words echoing in her mind. She pondered what to say to the Sahaf. Fahriye and Rashid chose to wait outside. A young woman opened the door. Despite her smooth skin and vibrant appearance, her shoulders were slightly slumped. Her light brown hair was tinged with gray. Her gaze swept over Azra's face.

"I'm here to visit Halil the Sahaf, and I bring greetings from Fahad the Pearl Seller," Azra announced.

"Just a minute," the woman whispered and disappeared, leaving the door ajar but not inviting Azra in. Murmurs drifted through it from within.

Azra leaned forward, squinting to peek through the crack. The walls were lined with shelves, and the scent of paper filled her nose.

A commanding male voice called out, "Come in at once."

The young woman reappeared at the door and gestured for Azra to enter. Halil was in a room facing the entrance. He wore reading glasses perched on the tip of his nose and scrutinized Azra with his small black eyes beneath a furrowed brow, clearly not pleased.

As he hastily straightened the pages and placed them on the coffee table beside him, he said, "I haven't seen the Pearl Seller in years. It must be something important for him to send you. What is it?"

The woman who had opened the door smiled as she poured tea for Azra and sat beside her.

"The Pearl Seller sent me. 'The Bookseller is my old friend,' he said, referring to you. Fahad entrusted you with a book many years ago. 'Halil will remember it,' he assured me. With your permission, I have come to retrieve it."

Halil straightened up. "*The Thread of Neptune*," he murmured, locking eyes with Azra.

Azra removed a carved wooden box from her bag, "He also asked me to give this to you."

Halil accepted the box, saying, "Excuse me for a moment," before exiting the room.

"We haven't met," said the young woman who had opened the door. "I am Sahaf Halil's daughter, River."

Azra, finding the introductions slightly forced, replied, "Nice to meet you, I'm Azra."

After a brief pause, River continued, "I've heard rumors about the Pearl Seller, but I didn't know of his friendship with my father. He doesn't share secrets."

"The absence of Aegean brought Fahad and me closer. Otherwise, I, too, mostly knew about him from the legends. After the fire in the Mossy Village, we were desperate."

"Aegean's absence and the fires... Every day, we face a new tragedy. The world has become a strange place," River observed, her gaze lingering on Azra's hair. "Still, it seems no breath thieves have visited your part of the world. That's a good sign."

"Breath thief?" Azra inquired, but before she could get a clear answer, Sahaf Halil re-entered the room. When Halil handed the book to Azra, her heart raced. She hadn't expected to receive *The Thread of Neptune* so quickly.

"For years, I've protected this book as if it were my own," Halil confessed. "I knew it would eventually leave my care, but I never imagined that time would come. Do you know how it ended up with Fahad?" he queried.

Azra nodded, reluctant to delve into details or reveal how much she knew.

"If you know the book's past, then you must comprehend its value. It's priceless, more valuable than Fahad's pearls. I trust you will take good care of it." A flicker of jealousy crossed Halil's eyes. Now a former bookseller, he found it hard to part with his books and entrust them to others. He would have preferred dealing with Fahad directly, but the engraved box mollified him slightly. After Azra's departure, he planned to examine the manuscript hidden inside.

"Don't misunderstand me," Azra stated, "I am merely an

intermediary. I must deliver it to its rightful owner. I won't keep you any longer. Perhaps we'll meet again in better times."

River escorted her to the door and, before closing it, clutched Azra's arm. "I'm not done yet. Meet me tomorrow, before noon, at Kamasis Beach. Don't leave this city without knowing about the breath thief," she whispered, then shut the door without waiting for a response.

Outside, Rashid and Fahriye appeared relieved that Azra had returned successful. Rashid, his shoulders sagging with fatigue, straightened his posture. They all yearned to return home. Dinner passed in silence until Azra brought up "the breath thief," prompting Rashid and Fahriye to exchange startled glances. "The Sahaf's daughter mentioned it. I don't understand, but she wants to meet tomorrow. 'Don't leave without knowing,' she insisted."

Hesitating, Rashid advised, "If you're meeting tomorrow, then listen to what Halil's daughter has to say. She knows more than us."

"I also want you to know," Fahriye interjected, "that the thief never visited our home. Rashid and I were on Glass Island when the sea receded. By the time we arrived in Kamasis, the thief had already left. It was too late by then." She nervously fiddled with her fork. If we had arrived sooner, we could have stopped him.

"How could we have known," Rashid reflected. "They say every cloud has a silver lining. Being here might have spared us from worse outcomes. No one has found a solution yet. Neither could we."

Confused, Azra had no choice but to wait patiently for tomorrow's meeting.

River

RIVER RESEMBLED, PROVERBIALLY, A TRICKLING stream that had once flowed with a roar but now had its water receding. Likewise, a little rain or a little snow would have revived her. But River had always had bad luck. When she put her auburn hair in a bun, her face became even more apparent. She separated a lock of white from the bun, wrapped it around her thumb, and waited. When the hair came loose from her finger, it bounced and swayed back and forth. Azra watched her. A few white strands were visible among her bushy hair, but none were as white as the lock of wavy hair hanging from the side of her forehead. River had liked Azra from the first moment she saw her, had recognized her anxious gaze as her own, and had told the traveler, what had happened when the Breath Thief had stepped into the city.

They sat on a rock along the beach, close to the bench where Azra had sat with Elmados months ago. In the old days, the waves would have crashed against the embankment where they dangled their feet, and the furious spray would have soaked them. Now, they were staring into a deep drop. A few pieces of garbage and other litter discarded by the locals mingled with the crab shells and pebbles at the bottom. The skeletal remains and rubbish on the shore emitted a decaying odor.

"We'll soon get used to the smell," River said, looking down the cliff. The two women would have been hurt badly if they had fallen, but they wanted to sit here anyway, preferring to talk and think of endless sea blue, imagining the sound the waves once made as they crashed against the rocks. River wrapped the white fringe lock of hair hanging along the side of her head around her finger. As she spoke, she repeatedly let it loose and re-wrapped it around her finger, doing it out of an old habit, as if she didn't even realize she was doing it.

"Aegean had not yet left; people had not thought of ever leaving Kamasis. My father wanted to expand his shop and tried various ways, and when that didn't work, he devised other schemes. I have been at his knee since I was a child. I grew up following him through the book aisles, noting what sold well and informing our patrons of new arrivals. My world consisted of books and my father. I vaguely remember my mother's face. She succumbed to her weak constitution. I can't remember the day she died or much from when she lived; I was so young. Whenever I needed my mother, I would run to my aunts.

"One day, while sitting across from each other in the shop, my father said, 'Our business is good; we have many customers. Many of them come from distant cities. This is what book addiction looks like. You travel to faraway lands to find a single manuscript. But it would be foolish for us to try and expand our business in Kamasis, River. Let's get out of here,' he said, 'let's move to the City of Sahaflar. You've never been there, but I'm sure you'll love it,' he insisted. It was as if we had switched roles. As if he was the child and I was the parent. He took me by the arm and led me to the front of the shop, 'Imagine this street full of booksellers. Not coppersmiths nor herbalists, just bookshops and lots of customers...' It wasn't hard to convince me. I shared his dreams and started preparing myself for a new beginning."

River ran her fingers over the rough surface of the rock they were sitting on and spoke without looking at Azra, "We had prepared everything, Azra, everything. But all these memories are from before that sinister thief came to haunt Kamasis." She made a fist and struck the rock.

"Did he steal your books?" Azra asked.

"No," said River, "He stole our breaths. First, he haunted our dreams. He wandered the most intimate streets of our dreams and asked us for help like a beggar or a needy old man. He appeared in them and repeated the same sentence, 'Give me a breath to live.' Our dreams turned into nightmares. We started complaining about insomnia, but at first, we didn't pay much attention. Incense was burned in houses, prayers were said, and that was it. We thought it would go away. How could we have known that the thief had his eyes on the very air that kept us alive? Who had even heard of such a thief before?"

Azra unconsciously squeezed the rock she was sitting on with both hands. She felt dizzy when she looked down from the cliff. River's words echoed in her brain. It was as if her lips were moving too slowly, and the echoes from thoughts in her head were gradually turning into a high-pitched ringing. Azra turned her head towards the bench where she had once sat with Elmados. A stone sat in her throat that she could not swallow.

River grabbed her shoulder and asked, "Are you okay?"

"I'm fine," Azra said, suddenly rising from her seat. But her body was still sitting next to River.

River asked again, "Are you okay?" She sensed something strange in Azra, but she could not understand what was happening to her.

"I'm fine," Azra repeated from where she stood up, but River didn't see her standing. Her soul and body had separated. It was as if her corpse was still sitting on the rocks. Azra was afraid of dying. She started breathing fast and panicked. Azra began to think that she would lose her breath, too. She looked towards the cliff and breathed in and out, but this time deeper and slower. When she had calmed down a little, she sat down. Her body and soul came back together again. Azra felt her chest with her hands. Something was missing. She felt an emptiness next to her heart. A deep hole had opened where her soul should be.

River's lips continued to move, and Azra could hear her voice, albeit faintly. But the ringing in her ears made it difficult for her to understand what she was hearing. This time, River grabbed her shoulders with both hands and shook her, "What happened? What's wrong?"

"Nothing," Azra could only say, "You go on."

"Not only did the ghost haunt me and my father, but he infiltrated the nooks and crannies of the city. He filled us like poisonous air. First, he turned our dreams into nightmares, then our lives into ruins. He carried a sack with him, hiding his shadowy face beneath his gray robe. He needed our breath to live. From sunrise to the next sunrise, he stole every breath we took. The thief took one day from each of our lives, not distinguishing between the young or old, all for itself. We had a hard time making sense of what we were going through. I didn't share my dreams with anyone at first. We were already in the process of moving; we were busy. But one morning, I was sitting at home and saw him in the room.

'I want to live,' he said, 'give me some of your breath.'

Death was standing in front of me. I thought of running away, but where could I hide? How far could I run? I was lucky to be on the ground floor. I jumped out of the open window. Yet somehow, he caught me as I ran across the yard and out into the street, his cold fingers I found around my neck. The thief grabbed my throat with one hand and, with the other, took out a glass container from his sack. 'Blow in it,' he commanded.

I wanted to scream, 'Help!'his fingers would hardly let me breathe even, much less scream. Under that gray robe was a ravenous monster hungry for life. Kicking it was useless. It had taken me over with its body as heavy as a stone.

'Blow,' he held the glass container to my lips. When he saw that I stopped protesting, his fingers around my neck relaxed. My lips touched the rim of the vessel, and I blew slowly and fearfully as if my soul was leaving my body. There was no escape from Death. Everything became dark. I don't know how long I lay unconscious in the garden, against the wall. When I opened my eyes, I thought I was as good as dead, gone. An uncanny silence hung over the garden. It took me a while to believe I was alive. I was breathing deeply, looking at my hands, surprised I could move. That day, I fell into the grip of a fatigue that I think will never leave me. It took me a while to realize that my hair had turned white. I didn't want to look in the mirror. I couldn't move my arm.

My father had it worse than me. We were both mistaken, thinking we had met Death himself . Of course, we didn't know from which hell that abomination came from. The exhaustion and pain he left behind killed our dream of moving. Like a fleeting dream, the City of Sahaflar disappeared into the darkness of our memory. Now, moving to another place seemed impossible. We tried to make up for what the thief had taken from us. But eventually, my father closed up the bookshop and retreated to our home. I had no power to help him. That demon ruined the lives of the people of Kamasis. Every day, he visited a different house, and everyone knew there was no escaping him. I'm telling you this to keep you on your guard. You intend to go on a long journey. You come from a village I don't know. The Pearl Seller has trusted you with an important responsibility. Otherwise, my father wouldn't so easily give that precious book he'd been holding for years to someone he'd only met for the first time. But rest assured, Azra, you don't have to do anything. Don't let your breath be stolen. You can turn back."

Azra wasn't sure if the fog was descending on Kamasis again or if it had only descended upon her eyes. She was frozen. She thought about jumping off the cliff. Azra wanted to smash the bench where she and Elmados had once sat, and to hug River and cry. She didn't move for a while. Then the words came out of her mouth, "I will go, River. I will do my best to bring back the waves of Aegean. I carry a small spark of hope. I can't go back and wait to die when the place where I live is disappearing day by day. As for what was stolen from you, I don't know what can replace them. Do you know where the thief is now?"

"I don't know," River said, twisting the lock of white hair on her forehead around her finger again, "He took what he wanted and left. He probably has his eye on other crowded cities where life is vibrant. But that's just a guess. You should always be on your guard. Don't be surprised if he shows up." She untangled the hair around her finger again. "And run."

A little rain and snow could bring River back to her old self and help her fulfill the dreams she had built with her father. However, she needed more time to regain her old strength. Until then, she would trickle, like a stream in drought.

Azra said goodbye to Sahaf's daughter. As she walked back to where she was staying, her spirit followed from behind. With her pale skin, pensive eyes, and the despair surrounding her mind, her body was like a fresh corpse that had not cooled down. She stared into the fog that had suddenly descended on the city and headed towards the Kandil Slope. The ringing in her ears had not yet subsided. On the slope in the fog, the house Fahriye had mentioned the day before appeared. A silhouette was visible in the window facing the street; it must be Captain Reza, she thought. He was wearing a khaki cardigan, his brown eyes fixed on Azra like two immovable stones. His gaze was not very hospitable, with his tense lips as thin as a knife. His white hair suggested that the Breath Thief had visited him, too. Azra continued walking up the slope without pausing, all the while keeping her eyes on the window. His wife appeared behind Captain Reza. From a distance, she didn't seem to be a fussy woman, and her motherly demeanor brought a smile to Azra's lips. She had only known her for two days, but Azra thought she could trust her. She and the captain were watching Azra. She wondered where their children, who sold fruit in the summer, were now. She could easily ask Fahriye if she wanted to. When she reached the end of the slope and arrived at Rashid's house, she knocked on the door and turned around. Her spirit had caught up with her body. The couple behind the window continued to stare at her through the fog until Fahriye opened the door.

"What a strange couple. They watched me the whole time as I walked up to the house," Azra stated as she entered.

"Who?" asked Fahriye, "Captain Reza and his wife? I told you;their fate threw them to a place they never expected. Anyway, we didn't want to sit at the table before you came. Come."

Even though savory aromas drifted through the house, a heavy stone sat in Azra's stomach. It was difficult to breathe. "I'm not hungry," she said and went upstairs. She entered her room and sat at the end of the bed. "Don't get used to this place, Azra," she murmured to herself, looking around.

She paused for a moment and said, "A breath thief, huh?" She swallowed. The young traveler opened the closet where she had placed her belongings. She had put the book she had gotten from Sahaf Halil there. Now, Azra was ready to set off. She started to pack her suitcase. If she prepared this evening, it would be easier to handle tomorrow's work. A navy-blue silk pouch caught her eye. She picked it up, felt through the contents, and then sat down on the floor and untied the package's knot. The contents fell out onto the carpet: dried hawthorns and a penknife. She picked up the penknife and examined it carefully.

Before her eyes, she saw a ship that had failed to reach the sea. She met her own eyes in the reflection of the sharp steel. Disappointed, tired, and exhausted. She touched the sharp point of the penknife to her right arm, and it cut through skin thinly. A harmless trickle of blood ran slowly down her arm to her hand. She could not hold back the tears.

As she brought the penknife near her wrist, she was startled by a scream, "What do you think you're doing?" She hadn't realized that Fahriye had quietly entered the room. Fahriye was staring in horror and anger at the blood running down Azra's arm. With a sudden movement, she put the plate of food she was bringing next to the bed and wrapped the meal's dinner cloth around Azra's arm, "Are you crazy?"

"I wish I was crazy." Azra paused, wiping the tears from her eyes with the back of her hand, and said, "I brought the Breath Thief to Kamasis. But I didn't know he would covet your breath. I helped him to find life. I thought he would journey on to find the answer to his question. Turns out he was nothing but a demon who should burn in flames."

Fahriye took Azra's head between her hands and wiped her tears with her thumbs, "Look at me, Azra," she said, "Snap out of it. Do you think cutting your wrist with that damn penknife will kill the Breath Thief? Your death won't stop him. You can only do something if you live. Follow the Pearl Seller's path. Find Lilith first. You can worry about the Breath Thief later. Go on, eat. I brought a plate of food. Come down if you want more." She kissed Azra's cheek.

Fahriye took the penknife with her when she left the room. The cloth wrapped around Azra's arm was stained with blood. The tremor in her body had not yet passed.

"No one invited me to dinner."

She put the hawthorn berries back in the navy-blue pouch on the floor, took the dinner plate, and sat on the bed. Azra reluctantly took a spoonful of food from the plate and put it in her mouth. The delicious taste of apples and potatoes made her forget everything. She had another spoonful.

CHAPTER SIX

Lilith Woke Up Many Years Ago

CENTURIES AGO, A CASTLE WAS built on the summit of an island, first conceived in the imagination of a king whose bones now mingled with the earth. The other rulers, adorned with golden crowns, burned with jealousy upon hearing of the castle's existence. The envious eyes of enemy soldiers melted as they gazed at the fortress's massive stone walls. But the king died. When his enemies met the same sad fate, the significance of the fortress diminished. The king's successors turned their backs on the nameless island in the middle of the sea, coveting glory elsewhere. The halls that once rang with songs of victory fell into silent desolation. Weeds overgrew the gardens where princesses once walked, tossing their tulle skirts. The gleaming swords of soldiers and the necklaces of queens faded from memory in the darkness of oblivion. The blood splattered on the stone walls of criminals condemned to death had long dried and blackened. The castle, which had come to life from a king's vision, had vanished into myth. Yet, it regained its true meaning once Lilith's graceful steps fell upon it.

When the birds returned to the earth and the world was at peace, Lilith awoke from her slumber underground. After bidding farewell to Simurgh, she chose this fortress as her sanctuary. The witch settled in the castle that had been erased from the memory of kings, never to leave it again. Over the years, she became synonymous with the island. The imposing structure was easily visible from every angle, giving the witch great opportunity to observe the islanders and their surroundings. However, the outer walls of the castle were high and held their secrets so well that it was difficult to discern what was happening inside. The stone walls separated the islanders from Lilith. Only when necessary would she disguise herself and mingle with the locals, a rarity for her. She preferred to live alone, under dim lights, and regarded the lives of the others with some disdain.

Unaware that Azra was approaching the island in a small ship, Lilith took her cards out of the oak box and began to shuffle them carefully, guided by old habits. Three cards caught between her fingers: a Ten of Wands, a Three of Swords, and a Chariot. The first card showed a picture of a young woman with her back turned. She was hunched over on her knees, with ten long sticks strapped to her back. The sticks extended beyond her height, tangling in her waist-length brown hair. She was looking towards the ground, exhausted.

"She must be a burdened woman," Lilith thought as her long, slender fingers moved over the Ten of Wands, "a stranger." She picked up the trio of swords. Three swords were stabbed through the bodies of two crows with their beaks raised upwards in pain. The card represented a wound. The witch ran her fingers across its black sky. The dead birds were entangled in black moss, and swords were covered in blood. Lilith moved on to the third card:

the Chariot. The Chariot, signaling ambition and travel, curled the witch's lips. "A charioteer who does not care for the reins," she murmured, "wearing a crown of laurel leaves in his hair." The horses' heads were pointing in different directions. "A rash novice who doesn't know what to expect."

Lilith turned her eyes from the cards to the window, to the sea. She squinted, suspecting a boat was hiding among the waves, a boat that would arrive on the island today or tomorrow. She wanted to see beyond the horizon. She got up from her desk and opened the lid of an iron cage at the foot of the bed. The scuffed old bird, which had forgotten how to use its wings due to its weariness of living in a cage, opened its tiny black eyes, which appeared between its blue plumage, in amazement. Lilith stroked the bird's head and, revived, it flew out the window into the sky. The kingfisher, with its long beak and bulging body, at first made short sprints through the air in joy of being free. It landed on the bastions of the castle, then again returned to the window. With a last look at its owner, it spread its wings wide and soared towards the sea. It flew between the waves for hours until it spotted the foreign ship sailing beyond the reach of the fishing boats.

First, it landed on the ship's bow. Its heart, unaccustomed to long flights, was beating fast. From there, it landed on the helm, controlled by a sailor named Gariban. Azra was asleep when it arrived. If she had known that a kingfisher was circling the ship doing Lilith's bidding, she would have jumped up and rushed up onto the deck. But she could only straighten her blanket and descend back into the vivid depths of her dreams.

The bird looked around, turning its cyan head from left to right. Gariban looked at the bird sideways without paying much attention. He lit the tobacco he had rolled and took a puff. The orange, fluffy body of the kingfisher was rising and falling because it had been flapping its wings for a long time. When the poor man blew the tobacco smoke towards the bird and steered to the left, the bird took wing and landed on the deck. The sounds it made as it walked on the wood resembled the rattling of rain; its wings rested while its delicate talons hurried over the boards. It fixed its small, black eyes on a metal bucket. After tilting its head to the right and looking for a while, it landed on the edge of the bucket with a few wing flaps and dipped its long beak into the bucket of water. When it lifted its head, water was pouring out of its beak.

It jumped on deck again and walked around as if to feel the ship. For a while, it did not use its tired wings. Then, it flew down the stairs and stopped in front of the cabin door. It poked its little head through the ajar door and looked inside. Azra had fallen asleep hours ago. After surveying the surroundings, the kingfisher flew towards the sleeping woman's body and hovered over her without waking her. Its claws were digging into her woolen dress. Azra did not seem to notice the bird hovering over her. For the first time in days, she was in a comfortable sleep. The bird landed on the table in the cabin, then on the porthole. Then, as if it had nothing else to do, it flew back through the ajar door and landed again on the edge of the metal bucket on the upper deck. It dipped its long beak into the water and looked up at Gariban.

The kingfisher could only see the sailor's back. Gariban had already run out of tobacco. A gray scarf was under his navy-blue coat, and the sailor's cap on his head shadowed his pierced dark face. An old scar on his right cheek distorted the symmetry of his face, while his slanted eyes disappeared under thick black eyebrows. The sailor's hands were still on the ship's helm; it was unclear whether he had noticed the bird's presence. Then, the bird turned its eyes to the waves and, with stealth, spread its wings and took off into the sky, disappearing into the endless blue. The boat seemed as if it could be sunk at any moment amid the foaming waves, defying the stubborn sea, moving up and down on the water.

The kingfisher, soaring through the air, flew back in the direction it had come from, landed on Lilith's windowsill, and looked inside. The room was dimly lit by the candle scones along its stone walls, and an auburn-skinned woman with straw-blonde hair falling over her shoulders was sitting at a table in front of the window, watching the sea and taking notes on paper. The bird flew to her shoulder and sang for a long time, all the while turning its blue head from side to side. The woman's hand stopped its writing. In the pause, the ink flowing from the tip of the pen started to form a large, expanding black dot on the yellowed page. She lifted her eyes from it, looked out to sea, and smiled. The witch then extended her ruby-ringed index finger towards the bird, and it jumped onto it from her shoulder.

She stroked the bird's blue head and said, "You brought the news I was waiting for."

The witch opened one of the drawers, took out a box, and opened its lid. The long, thin beak of the kingfisher dived in and grabbed a long worm, which, when stuck in the bird's beak, curled up like a rosary beetle. In one motion, the bird swallowed the worm whole. The witch stood up and went to the iron cage at the head of the bed.

"Get some rest," she whispered as she opened the cage, put in first the box of worms and then the bird, and closed it again. Her fingers ran through the cards once more and chose a new one: The King of Hearts. The wise man in the picture gazed calmly back at Lilith. A fish swam in the pool in front of the King of Hearts.

"Fahad," she murmured, "you must have sent her." She said it not as a prophecy but as a wish.

BY THE TIME AZRA OPENED her eyes, the bird was already back inside its cage. Being able to listen to the irresistible melody of waves once again brought refreshment to her parched soul.

Although the boat had been churning for days, she was lit up with a joy she had forgotten years ago. The fog that had obscured her vision and the uncertainty that still awaited her ahead were dissolving in the sea's cool mist. A few days ago, she had left Cam Island with Gariban. Azra was relieved when Raşit had intervened and vouched for Gariban, his closest mate. The thought of sailing with this tough-looking man who always hid his face under his hat did not appeal to the young woman.

The middle-aged childless couple waited on the beach until the boat had left the harbor, waving and shouting "Goodbye!" until the young woman and Gariban disappeared from sight.

AZRA MOVED A LITTLE CLOSER to the porthole in her cabin and looked out towards the waves. She closed her eyes and imagined them along the shores of the Mossy Village. She believed she could bring Aegean back to it with the pebbles of her village. The fires and the aridness of her land could not make her give in to despair. Her feet touched the water again. She had left Kamasis and the Ida Mountains behind. After an overnight stay in Narlı, guided by Fahad, Azra had arrived at the shores where the sea still washed up on the beach. Aegean took on a different look here. It continued to foam and ripple with enthusiasm as if it was not the one who had left her village. This recklessness hurt Azra—a mild pain, like the salty drops of water splashed on her injured arm, burning her skin. Aegean did not know what it was to miss something.

Azra rarely came out of her cabin, content to observe the sea through the porthole. She did not realize that Lilith was waiting for her. The journey she had taken with the strange sailor in a small ship had brought unexpected healing to her soul. Without ever touching land again, without anchoring in any harbor, she could spend the rest of her days among the waves, leaving everything behind. But Azra had to see Lilith. And she could not let Fahad down or betray his trust.

She had first encountered Lilith in Sevim's notes. The Pearl Seller's dealings with the witch and his trust in her were comforting. The young woman wondered how similar the Lilith she had imagined and the woman waiting for her would be. She was already trying to envision what she would say if they met. The one who had tasted the blood of the Simurgh and called the birds back to the world had also helped Fahad find his bearings. No one could guess how old she was or which lands she had seen. There was hardly anything written about her. The witch's talents went far beyond spell casting –she had also found ways to tame the black moss and make the people obey her. The Pearl Seller had left his story of Lilith incomplete. Perhaps if she could return Aegean to the Mossy Village, the witch herself would share the rest with Azra, accompanied by the familiar melody of the waves. The prospect of seeing her filled the young woman with anticipation and excitement. Yet she trusted her instincts and keen eyes and wanted to reserve judgment as to what kind of woman Lilith was.

Azra went out onto the deck to watch the sunset. Gariban was a silent man, and Azra appreciated those familiar with the language of silence. Her hair blew in the wind, and she still struggled to keep her balance as she walked around the ship. After the sun had fallen, she found a place to lay down, threw a blanket over herself, and fell asleep on deck, watching the stars. The nightmares had haunted her during the night, and sleeping on the planks of hardwood had caused a terrible ache in her bones. When she opened her eyes, dawn had broken, but the sun had not yet risen. Her back and shoulders were stiff. For a while, she had difficulty moving her neck. With immense gratitude, she accepted the warm cup of tea that Gariban offered her.

She realized that the boat was not sailing.

The silent sailor spoke as if to explain, "The night became foggy, and I was sleepy, so I thought I'd anchor the ship and get some rest." He slowly pulled up the chains of the anchor stuck in the sand.

Azra responded to Gariban with silence. She trusted him and took a sip of her tea. The warmth spreading down her throat was enough to soothe her pain. They expected to reach the island before the sun reached its highest. The skillful sailor's calculations were accurate, and it was not yet noon when the castle's bastions appeared on the horizon. Azra spent the last hours observing the castle, trying to unravel the island's mystery. The closer she got to land, the larger Lilith's castle grew, transforming into an insurmountable creature in her eyes.

The Fire Vinegar

THEY ANCHORED ALONG THE BEACH near the castle rather than in the island's main harbor. It would be easy to reach its gate and avoid the locals from there. Azra was drenched in sweat when the ship finally arrived and retreated to her cabin, where she changed her clothes and tidied her hair. She put her beret on her head. The poor sailor was waiting for her outside. When the sea became shallow, he laid anchor, and they both got into the ship's small dinghy. Gariban rowed them ashore. Where the waves started to crash, he jumped into the water and pulled the boat up onto the beach. They were near the outer wall surrounding the castle.

"You know where to find me," the sailor said, "I will not leave the island until I hear from you."

"Understood," Azra said, not knowing where to turn her eyes. Setting foot on the ground again after days made her dizzy. Although she wasn't moving, it still felt like it, as if the sands were swaying like the sea.

"You're obviously not used to long cruises," Gariban said with a wry smile.

Azra felt nauseous.

"In a few hours, you will get used to the serenity of land again." He bowed his head in farewell and walked towards the boat.

Azra wanted to respond, but her stomach stopped her. She lay on the beach for a while without moving. Cold sweat accumulated on her forehead; she was cold. She closed her eyes and listened to the rhythm of the waves, which she knew by heart.

A light breeze blew, carrying a soothing woman's voice to Azra, "Welcome."

She sat up and opened her eyes.

The wind that had said "Welcome" was circling the shoreline with bits of grass in its wake. She looked towards the outer walls of the tower. Ahead, she could see the bastions of the castle but no other details. Azra started down a path that led from the beach inland to the forest. Along the way, she passed an islander on his way to the sea.

"Don't follow the shadow, stranger," warned the middle-aged man as he grasped Azra's arm. "I don't know who you are or where you came from, but there's a witch who lives in that castle in the distance, and I'm certain you're vulnerable enough to fall into her traps—who hasn't? I lost one of my children to the forest. I still search for his soul. Stick to the path. Be deaf to the whispering wind; her voice is poisonous. It will clasp around your neck and not let go and you'll become ensnared in this forest forever, lost to time itself. Her ghosts who think the forest is their nest are more powerful than you can imagine. One day, I will watch her burn until nothing remains—not even a fragment of bone or a strand of hair. One day, Lilith will meet her end, and it will be before I breathe my last."

The wind interrupted his speech, but it did not whisper this time. It was cold, cold enough to make Azra shiver.

The man's grip slowly loosened. He repeated, "Do not follow the shadow, stranger," and disappeared into the forest's depths.

"Which shadow, what wind?" Azra was confused, but nobody responded her this time.

Undaunted, she walked towards the path through the forest leading up to them. If she followed the map Fahad had drawn, she would reach the main gate in half an hour. The wooded road, though broad, was full of shadows. The faint rays of the winter sun were diminished by the trees. She touched their red-barked, damp trunks. Azra walked slowly and tried to decipher the language of the woodland, listening intently for small creaks and whisper-like sounds.

She stopped when the road forked in three different directions in front of her.

"Those who follow see everything," the wind whispered.

The map in her hands showed that she should follow the path to the left, but she could hear footsteps upon the center one. The dark road that curved to the right looked sinister.

"Don't you wonder where your nightmares are hiding? You can't carry them for the rest of your life."

She ignored the whisper of the wind. She assumed that if she ignored it, the whisper would disappear, and decided to take the middle path and find the footsteps. Then, she would turn back and head for the castle.

Unaware that she would be caught in the sinister webs of her past, she quickened her pace along the second path. Further along, she was glad to find a man walking in the distance, not knowing that she had fallen into the ambush of her nightmares.

But not wanting to leave caution completely to the wind, she kept silent and slowed down, and by concealing herself behind the wide trunks of the trees, she began to follow him at a distance. The shadows of the branches fell on the stranger, transforming him into a vague figure that was hard to make out. However, Azra sensed something familiar in all this confusion. She felt a closeness to the stranger ahead whose face she could not yet see. Nevertheless, she knew better than to trust such a man blindly. She couldn't afford to be swayed by mere intuition. As she observed him, keeping her distance, the stranger turned down another path and continued walking until he came in front of a small house.

Azra hid amongst the trees while he knocked on the door and waited. Before she could see who opened the door, the man entered. Azra slunk through the garden and went up to the window, careful and hesitant, barely daring to breathe. She wanted to see the people inside and find out if she could trust them. Then, she would be able to knock on the door. Azra dreamed of spending time with them, to have someone to talk to and confide in.

But when she saw the stranger's face, she cried out in a startled voice, "Dad!" She was not aware of her own sound.

The man's dark eyes met Azra's as he looked toward the cry. His gaze had not changed in all these years.

New disappointments seemed to be added to the tiredness he always carried. Next to him was a middle-aged woman who looked a little younger than him with a baby clinging to her skirt. A brother she didn't know existed and a stepmother she had never met. Suddenly, the baby's innocent eyes and the woman's questioning gaze locked onto Azra. As she ran away without looking back, she did not notice the invisible nets wrapping around her arms. She had fallen into the trap of her insidious memories.

"You can't heal by ignoring it."

Azra was so mortified that she didn't notice the wind caressing her face.

She had not seen her father since the day he had left home, vanishing. The lips of the man, who had become increasingly silent with the death of her mother, were sealed against Azra. He had wanted to take his daughter with him when he left the Mossy Village, but when he could not convince her to come, he had set off alone. The young woman continued to live, ignoring these ominous memories. She was surprised when she suddenly saw her father. She would not go to the door and talk to the man who had never even once returned to the Mossy Village to see her. He had obviously erased his daughter from his life. Azra regretted that she had strayed from the path Fahad had shown her. She would never forgive herself for following him to that house.

She returned to the forest path, trying to erase what she had seen from her memory. She needed to find the fork in the road again but had lost her place on the map. It did not show all the trail's windings. Breathing in and out, she tried to calm herself and stopped to take in her surroundings. There was only one road ahead of her. If she followed it and not go any deeper into the forest, it might be easy to find the fork in the road. There was a crunch behind her. Was it her father? She was scared to death at the thought. No, she wouldn't look back.

"How did you get here?" a familiar voice touched her shoulder.

There was silence.

"What do you want?"

"I want you to disappear!"

The voice behind her suddenly stopped.

That it did stop made Azra even angrier at her father. She turned around and shouted desperately to the vaporizing figure, "If you want to talk, you know where to find me."

"You can't destroy your father with the smoke of anger."

Azra swept her hand through the air before her as if to brush away and silence the wind that swirled around her.

She came to a place where the map she had held showed her where she was. If she got lost in memories again, she would never find the castle; she would suffer forever in the forest of whispers. Fahad's friendly handwriting on the map calmed her. She imagined the Pearl Seller's blue eyes hiding the sea within them.

As he left, he put his hand on Azra's shoulder and said, "Your meeting with Lilith will not be easy. You must be careful of her traps. If you are not strong enough, she will crush you like a small, black insect and will not hesitate to drink your blood. Overcome her tricks, and you will earn her respect. Remember, what you learn from her will help you see the world differently. Lilith is not your enemy."

She sensed that the shadowy figure from the darkness of her past had not come to her by chance. As Azra walked back the way she had come, she was careful not to look behind nor to listen to the whispers that filled her ears. When she returned to the fork in the road, the young woman breathed a sigh of relief.

"Go deeper. If you want to be reborn, then kill."

A gray-robed figure appeared to the right of the forked road. His dark face, hidden under his hood, could not be seen. He looked like the Breath Thief. Azra looked back at the map in her hand as if asking for help. Ignoring the dark figure waiting at the beginning of the third path, she followed the path drawn by the Pearl Seller. After some time going down it, she could faintly make out the castle's walls behind the trees. Azra forced herself not to look back. She could not face the Breath Thief now. The possibility that he might be Elmados frightened her heart.

Azra prayed that provocative visions would not come her way again. Evening was falling when she arrived in front of the main gate. As she entered and followed Fahad's path, she became dizzy again and paused. Azra climbed the stairs of the castle and reached the great hall. She could hardly control her trembling knees. In the center of the hall was an empty banquet table. The table was already set with delicious looking food, but there was no one in the hall.

"Welcome."

Azra immediately recognized the female voice carried by the wind. When she spun around to see its owner, she was torn between fear and curiosity. Lilith's straw-blonde hair, green eyes reminiscent of fireflies, and thin smiling lips were enough to mesmerize Azra. She sensed a friendly demeanor in her, but there was an uncanny ominousness in her voice. The fireflies in her eyes might go out at any moment. The witch was too experienced to be called young, too agile to be called old. Beauty was a charm that Lilith did not wish to lose. It was evident that she surrounded herself with this mysterious magic. The deceivingly youthful expression disappeared from Lilith's face.

She ran her long, slender fingers over Azra's face and said, "I greeted you with your dark side, your nightmares. Most people attempt to conceal them, but I prefer to reveal them. The way to heal pain is to touch it. If you run away, they turn first into black smoke, then into things much worse. The forest path is treacherous, and visitors complain that I am inhospitable. You'll realize this is a lie. If only they could heed the whispers of the wind, they might find their way, but first, they must master the voices in their minds."

Azra swallowed, not knowing what to say. Trying to gauge whether the woman she saw in front of her was a dream or a nightmare.

She spoke in the most polite way she could find, "Dear Lilith, I would not have had the courage to come to your door if I had not been lost in an endless nightmare. The world seems to be tired of spinning, and as it stumbles, it destroys those above it."

The memory of her father's dark eyes was an agony in her heart. She wanted to bury those forever, but even if she didn't like the witch poking around, she didn't want to show discontent. She fought not to let her soul fill with despair.

"I wanted to get to know you a little," Lilith's fingers trailed along the woman's chin, "You have sharp edges," she whispered, her green eyes boring into Azra's, "You are harsh to people who cross you. That's fine. But it would be better if you stretched your boundaries a little. Your desire to meet me outweighed your ambition to confront the Breath Thief." She removed her hand from Azra's chin. A small wave of doubt crossed her eyes, "Did Fahad send you?"

Azra nodded and said, "He said you knew the mysteries of black moss. You have unlocked many mysteries with it. Aegean has left our village! We watched with helpless eyes as the waves, day by day, abandoned our shores. The people despaired and migrated to distant lands. Our forest went up in flames. Fahad hopes you can find a solution." Her voice trembled. Her heart was racing, and Azra clasped her hands in front of her chest, squeezing her fingers.

Lilith paused and thought. Then she spoke, "I have never heard of Aegean leaving shores where it belongs. This is an unforeseen disaster.

It does not bode well. It is full of complications," she looked down. "But let's put that aside for now." Turning her gaze back to the young woman, Lilith continued, "You look worn out from the journey and your experience in the forest." She walked to the table, picked up the decanter, and poured a crimson-orange drink into a crystal goblet. "It's your first day. Get some rest." She handed the goblet to Azra. "Fire vinegar is healing for the soul."

Azra took the goblet. The sharpness of the vinegar burned her throat. The flames that filled her stomach spread throughout her body. Comforted by the pleasant aroma of orange and cinnamon, she finished the fire vinegar in one gulp.

The Cabinet of Herbs:
Wolf's Claw, Dragon's Blood, and Belladonna

AZRA SPENT THE NIGHT IN one of the rooms Lilith had offered her. The sound of waves filled her ears before she even opened her eyes. Upon waking, she rushed to the window to gaze at the sea before her, a sight she could hardly believe. The arid land she had left behind had drained her of everything she cherished. Now, the sea's spirit was sprouting fresh shoots in her soul.

She descended the stone stairs of the castle and found the hall deserted. The banquet table had been cleared, and there was no trace of humanity. With uneasy steps, she wandered through the corridors once graced by princesses with sweet pride and arrogance. In halls where kings had issued war decrees and orders that shattered peace treaties, Azra searched for the witch she had met the day before. The pleasant scent of amber and mimosa that had once filled the hall was now replaced by the sea's aroma. Lilith had mentioned the importance of listening to the wind, a skill Azra had yet to learn, and the unknown overwhelmed her with panic. She hurried through the dim corridors toward the kitchen.

The kitchen was a large space with a smoldering fireplace, messy countertops, and a cabinet of herbs with its door hanging open. Iron pots hung from the ceiling, and copper pots, tin cans, and bronze trays lined the cabinets. Dried corn and garlic bunches adorned the passage to the balcony, and jars with tightly sealed lids sat on the shelves, filled with colorful fluids, oils, and dried herbs.

A thin thread of smoke still rose from the fireplace's ashes, and the main counter was littered with ladles, greasy wooden spoons, and a warm iron cauldron. She approached the cabinet of herbs, where the names of strange spices were etched onto their glass bottles. She picked up a few and read the labels: "wolf's claw," "dragon's blood," and "belladonna." Curiously, she opened the lids and sampled the spices, sneezing at the unfamiliar scents.

"You have discovered the heart of the castle," came a voice behind her. Startled, Azra recapped one of the bottles she had picked up, but in her haste, she caused another one to fall, shattering the glass labeled "dragon's blood." The broken pieces were coated in a sticky red liquid.

"You must know what your fingers are touching," Lilith advised. "Learn to use the spices, and you'll find a cure. Otherwise, they can become a poison that mixes with your blood."

Azra looked up from the broken glass to see Lilith, unrecognizable at first. The old lady's graying hair and deep wrinkles starkly contrasted with the vibrant fireflies in her eyes. Before Azra could speak, Lilith scooped up some dragon's blood with her fingers, demonstrating its properties. "Red gum is collected from a special tree not native to these lands. The resin from dozens of trees fills just a small bottle,"

Lilith explained, tasting the gum. She handed Azra a dirty plate, instructing her to clean up the mess and then wash the resin in a strainer. "If you're not careful, years of work will go to waste."

"Lilith?" Azra asked, taking the plate.

"Yes, it's me. I'm too tired to cast the spell of youth every day. Without it, I age rapidly. Sometimes, I regret that there's no place for me in this fast-paced, selfish world. But don't worry, in a few days, I'll grow bored of this and return to my usual self."

"Yesterday, you had the figure of a princess..."

"And today, the profile of a witch." They laughed together. Lilith then lifted the lid of the warm cauldron and began stirring its contents with a wooden spoon. "I've long sensed something strange in Aegean. The sea creatures had become timid, as if they were avoiding the shores and refusing to leave the depths. Despite the storms, the waves lacked foam. I didn't realize that Aegean drew its waves from other, more ancient shores. I've prepared a mixture of Seal of Solomon seeds for you. So that I might assist, I need a clear mind, not beauty."

Azra said, "I've brought things from the Pearl Seller and Sevim. Fahad believes black moss might be part of the solution. Sevim says you brought the birds to earth. You've seen Simurgh with your own eyes."

Taking another spoonful of the Seal of Solomon's concoction, Lilith mused, "I was once almost out of life. If the birds hadn't left the earth, Simurgh would never have awakened. Sometimes, there's good in what seems evil and evil in what seems good. Without Simurgh's descent, I would have died. My corpse would have rotted in an underground cesspool. But that's all in the past. Fahad's intuition has never failed me. He may be right about the black moss, but I won't understand how to use it until I get to the problem's core." She poured a ladle of the mixture for Azra and herself.

Azra returned to her room and brought back the articles she had carried with her for Lilith: *The Thread of Neptune* book, a feather from Simurgh's wing, and the pearl necklace Fahad had given her. The fireflies in Lilith's eyes danced as she put on the necklace and flipped through the book's pages. "It's commonly known as 'black moss' or 'Neptune's thread.' It's a despised sea plant, overlooked by scholars and ignored by other witches. But the common folk know some of its mystery. I, too, have been ensnared in the tangles of this web. It's tricky; if it wraps around your feet, you can't escape, but if you're able to wield it, the world should fear you."

Lilith reminisced, "Fahad washed up on the island's shores clutching this book in his hand. He was young then. If he sent the necklace, he must have dived into the depths he had so desired."

She then fell silent, flipping through the book and humming occasionally, pacing back and forth around the kitchen as if searching for something. Azra watched her, expecting the witch to stop at any moment and provide a solution, but it never came.

Azra took a break and ventured into the garden. The shadowy forest paths again appeared beside her. The dense tree branches darkened the trail even more. Fearing the sight of her father, she turned her back on the woods, dreading the deceptions she might encounter. Instead, she headed for the beach, listening to the soothing sound of waves. Upon returning to the castle kitchen, she now found Lilith with a slightly hunched back. Her gray hair had turned white, and her lips had sunken into her mouth.

"Are you here? I was looking for you," Lilith said with a lisp, her newly missing teeth affecting her speech. "I mustn't neglect the beauty potion. I'm aging faster than I thought, but I'm out of primrose. Bring me a bunch from the morass in the forest, and I'll add it to the mixture."

And so, Azra found herself at the forest's edge again.

With her first step into it, the wind whispered, "You will have to swim in its muddy waters to appease the creature called the morass."

"I'm ready for anything as long as I don't meet the likeness of my father," Azra declared. She wanted to avoid getting lost in the forest's deceptions again. Following Lilith's directions, she walked briskly, ignoring the squirrels and brown rabbits that fled from hearing her approach. Eventually, she reached the morass, where the stunning pink flowers bloomed at the other edge of its waters. But to pluck the primrose, she first had to cross to the opposite shore. As she jumped into the swampy lake, a frog leaped in, and a green lizard dived into the bushes. The muddy water reached to her knees, but with each step, she sank deeper. By the time she reached the other shore, the morass was past shoulder height. She plucked the flowers and then heard a low growl.

"Don't look at the wolf," Lilith had warned. "You will be saved if you ignore it."

She turned back, holding the flowers high above her head, as the mud reached her neck.

"Take your time. If you panic, you will sink faster," the witch had said. Taking a deep breath, she reached the shore and ran back to the castle without looking behind her.

In the kitchen, Lilith instructed, "Wash the flowers well. Crush them in a mortar and then soak them in hot water." She handed Azra a jar with trembling hands. "Add the brewed tea to this mixture. I'm going to lie down for a while."

Azra followed the instructions precisely. As she stirred the herbal tea into the jar, the old woman lying down on a divan in the corner grew heavier by the minute, and her eyes closed. Memories of her mother flooded Azra's mind the morning she found her dead in bed. She froze, the hot jar nearly slipping from her grasp. An unbearable heaviness filled her chest, and she feared finding Lilith dead like her mother. Regaining control, she picked up the jar again and walked over to the witch, her tears falling into the mixture.

Kneeling by the couch, she fed the unconscious witch three spoonfuls of the potion. "Three spoons is enough," Lilith murmured, opening her eyes. "Old age is hard, my dear," she coughed as she rose from the couch. "Are you crying, crazy girl?" she teased. "You should have wept shamelessly. You think I have the eyes to die like this."

Azra smiled, recalling the childhood stories where tears held magic. "Healing is hidden in genuine drops," Lilith mused thoughtfully, looking at Azra as if seeing her for the first time in a long while. "You're covered in mud; run and change," she instructed, stretching and yawning. "It will take me a day to recover. But I can manage for now. Tomorrow, we'll see the real effect of the potion. I'll need three more spoonfuls before I go to sleep tonight. Are you still here? Go on, run!"

When Azra returned to the kitchen after changing, Lilith was busy at work. "You did better than I expected," she remarked. "The morass is a reckless creature. It only offers its flowers only to those who dare to swim in its unpleasant waters. It's a good sign that you risked it. Now we can put aside the primrose and the trials of old age," she said, disappearing into one of the castle's corridors.

Lilith returned, carrying some heavy books, with her face more vigorous and her hair regaining its original color. "I need to be sure of my memory and refresh my knowledge," she explained, leafing through the book on Neptune's thread. "I hate to make mistakes. At times like these, it's necessary to swallow my pride and revisit the old pages, dusting off the books," she continued, turning pages and sometimes muttering in amazement.

"How happy I was that Fahad brought this book when he escaped from the Island of the Monks. Smuggling books from that holy shrine was no small feat. Fahad offered me this book as a token of his ambition to learn. He wanted to gain my trust. It was nice that my experiments on the moss were written down giving me the credit. If only you knew, Azra, how many deceivers my old eyes have met, how many fame-thirsty people. I almost believed that no one left on earth knew how to appreciate things. Fahad was honest enough to destroy some of my misplaced beliefs."

"Posidonia Oceanica," she pronounced in a strange accent, "is a free spirit. A restless plant. A refuge for fish. A black forest hiding in the depths of the waters. Shady and dark, and therefore uncanny. Its rhizomes are insolent; they like to spread. It moves thoughtlessly, not caring where it's going. Neptune's grass is not as fond of its roots as any tree. It is unfaithful. It reminds one of the unseen. A deceitful plant." The witch ran her finger over the picture of the black moss in the book.

She went to the shelves opposite the counter and looked at the jars, selecting two and placing them on the counter. Opening one, she revealed some fresh moss with its roots intact. "The unique plant of the Mossy Village," said Lilith. "I prepared a protective potion and kept it in a glass jar to preserve its freshness." She took a white towel and carefully placed the plant on it, stretching its brown, hairy roots toward Azra. "Do you see it?"

Azra leaned in closer, her eyes wide. "The plant washes ashore in the fall. The dried leaves form little mounds there. When the rhizomes you mentioned dry, they burn crispy in the fire. Perfect for strengthening the flames," Azra explained, touching the wet leaves on the towel.

Lilith smiled approvingly and whispered, as if revealing a great secret, "Neptune's thread blooms every thirty years and the fruit washes ashore with the broken leaves." She unscrewed the lid of the second jar and spread a handful of berries on the dry side of the towel.

"These look like olives," Azra marveled.

"Sea olives," said the witch.

"No one has ever mentioned them to me."

“People can’t talk about things they don’t know.”

Taking one of them in her hand, Azra squinted and looked closer, asking, “Is it edible?”

“No, don’t try it. You can’t just pop it in your mouth. Sea olives are rare and rarely used. I suppose this fruit could bring Aegean back to where it belongs, but the situation is more complicated than I thought. Returning the tide will not be easy. I would like to consider one or two possibilities and come to a definite conclusion: Aegean is obviously angry about something. Not one, but many events have come together to cause her to withdraw into herself. If we do not intervene, it may disappear permanently from your village and possibly other places as well. I need some time,” she said, squinting at one of the olive pellets between her fingers. She closed the books and stacked them. Her straw-blonde hair shimmered in the fading light of sunset as she placed the plant and sea olives back into the jars.

THE WAX MELTED UNDER THE intensity of the flames. Lilith measured two teaspoons each of rosemary and wormwood oils, carefully dribbling them into the bubbling wax. The steam from the boiling concoction gently caressed Azra's face. Lilith removed the hot crucible from the fire, setting it aside to cool. After letting it cool some, she poured the ointment from it into a small glass bottle. The liquid, taking the shape of the container, solidified instantly.

Lilith scooped up a warm dollop of the ointment with her finger, extended it towards me, and daubed on my lips, saying, "To find your voice."

CHAPTER SEVEN

The Cry of the Roots

I SMILED AS THE WARMTH of the ointment spread through my body. Tomorrow, I would set off.

As I left the island, the various glass vials of potions, ointments, and oils in my bag clinked against each other with the rocking of the waves, emitting musky scents. I knew that inside the ever-diminishing castle lived two women, like day and night, their transforming bodies belonging to one soul. Lilith could change herself into any illusion. I was certain I would return to that wretched castle someday. My gaze lingered on the shadowy forest. The thought of encountering the dark-eyed man again, who had taken the eerie form of my father, filled me with dread. Even if it was just an illusion created by Lilith's whispers, it had been enough to frighten me. The guardian wolf of the morass peaked its head out from the underbrush as our ship was leaving the shore. It had not forgotten that I had plucked the primroses. Its wild gaze fixed on me; it could have leaped at me in one move, but something held it back.

I watched as the silhouette of the castle blended into the horizon.

When the sea met the sky at the horizon, I leaned back and looked at Gariban at the helm. I was eager to tell him what I had seen in the castle, about the witch's straw-colored hair, her eyes reminiscent of fireflies. He was staring out to sea, lost in thought. The sailor had asked me to board immediately without even asking how I was, eager to leave the strange place. Gariban was not the right person to share my stories with. I dropped the idea.

My anxious heart raced in my chest the whole voyage back until reaching the Mossy Village. As I walked down the main street, the bottles in my bag clinking against each other, the loneliness of the abandoned houses darkened my spirit. The branches of my fig tree had not yet budded. The garden, neglected in my absence, was filled with dry leaves. I entered my home like a stranger; the inside was a bit colder than usual. Fahad and Sevim, unaware of each other, were waiting for my return. I had filled the absence of Aegean with their stories. Now, it was my turn to share mine.

I was the one who had knocked on Sevim's door, announcing my return. When the Pearl Seller learned of my arrival, he came immediately to my home. Their faces, blended with curiosity and fear, were eager to feel a spark of hope. I told each of them my story. I did not want to forget the witch's advice; the more I spoke, the more I remembered.

"I was almost getting used to living in the castle," I concluded.

"I felt the same way," Fahad replied.

"If you had stayed there, you would have left us to decay," Sevim sighed.

"I've brought bottles clinking in my bag, filled with potions made by Lilith," I stated, "and I will call the sea back to where it belongs."

The new crescent slowly withdrew from the evening sky, and the sparkling stars came a little closer, offering little light to illuminate my path.

"Wait for the moon to withdraw," Lilith had said. "At that time, a door opens deep into the earth. It is an old belief. Go to the place where the sea has receded and bury the black moss olive in the sand. Offering the sea fruit to Aegean will calm its anger. The olive is a very ancient declaration of peace. Let it rest for a while under the thin light of the new moon. But that is not enough."

I had waited fourteen days for it to transform into a full moon. Time was like a tensely drawn bow. I was afraid, yet I wanted to trust Lilith's prophecies. As the new moon grew larger each night, I made my final preparations.

"When the full moon rises, the waters will rise again," Lilith said. "The intensity of the tide will cause the sea to throw its waves onto the shore. Our plea will loosen the tight reins it holds, directing its waves towards your village."

At last, the fourteenth day arrived. The sun set, and the full moon rose calmly in a reddish glow. Some rain clouds had appeared in the sky. The moon, swiftly moving behind the shroud of the speeding clouds, appeared and disappeared, sometimes hiding its light from us for minutes. Ignoring the thunder, I went to the shore. The bonfire I had prepared was ready to blaze, but the storm intensified, and the wind made it difficult for me to walk. The Pearl Seller arrived first; together, we struggled to light the fire. The wind seemed fixated on extinguishing the flames, and no matter what we did, it wouldn't allow the fire to come to life. Lightning flashed somewhere in the distance. Fahad's face lit up with hopelessness. Darkness seemed about to swallow us under the fading light of the full moon. The sky thundered angrily, and a raindrop fell on my nose. Then another.

"It won't happen," said Sevim. Her mood was grim, "You're wasting your time." In the distance, lightning fell behind Mount Ida, illuminating the old woman's despairing face. Her dim eyes were grey, and her frail body could have collapsed to the ground at any moment under her thick coat. In her condition, she resembled an ominous ghost from the other world.

The thin branch I held in my hand to light the fire snapped, crackling between my fingers. I had called Sevim here tonight. A spark of regret twinkled inside me. "The fire will burn tonight. If not, we'll move to another place away from the rain."

Fahad looked up at the sky, "It looks like the rain will only sprinkle a few drops and then withdraw," he agreed.

Sevim took her hands out of her pockets as if she didn't want to bother with us, "Alright, alright," she said. "Why don't we stand close together to form a shield from the wind so that we can start the fire?"

The storm howled through us. Shoulder to shoulder, we bent down to form a human wall and patiently waited for the feeble flames to revive. The storm was beating at our backs, and lightning continued to strike the distant mountains. Despite the foreboding night, we managed to strengthen the fire. We watched in silence as the blazing flames came to life. Sevim, wanting to warm her hands, had tucked them into the pockets of her thick, navy-blue coat and moved closer to the fire. In the chilled air, her breath turned white, emanating from her mouth, making her look older and more worn than ever. The wind had disheveled Fahad's hair, but otherwise, he looked fine. He hadn't lost hope.

As they watched, I placed Simurgh's feather into the middle of the flames. Sevim wasn't expecting this. She straightened up in surprise, her eyes open wide, forgetting the bone-chilling wind. She watched the feather amongst the flames.

"'What belongs to Simurgh must return to Simurgh,'" Lilith had said. She had carved three letters onto a dry olive branch:

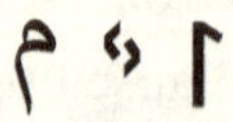

"Burn the branch with the feather. Do not interfere with the flames. Let them sway as they wish, and allow them to die out when the time is right. The water must find the peace it lost. Beings of the earth must return to where they belong. Their serenity will also appear amongst people."

Simurgh's feather resisted the flames. Its colorful feathers sparkled in the intensity of the heat. Then, succumbing, it caught fire. The fire had also sparked anxiety within Sevim's heart. It was clear she did not want to lose the treasure she had found years ago. I placed my hand on her shoulder. Tears had gathered in her eyes. The feathers continued to shimmer and scatter sparks in the intensity of the fire.

Then, all at once, Simurgh's great wings emerged from the middle of the blaze. The burning feather turned black and to ash, and the bird, breaking free, soaring above the void left by the sea.

Sevim, reaching out with her hands towards the great bird, shouted, "Did you see? There He flies."

We fell into stunned silence, not daring to speak. Looking back down, the flames had died out. The three of us locked our gazes on the smoking ashes.

But Fahad couldn't stand it, "The rest is up to God," he muttered, "A drop of His mercy can turn desolate deserts into seas." He cleaned his ash-covered hands by wiping them on some stones on the ground. Lightning again struck the distant mountains. The sky rumbled. The moon, hidden behind the clouds was about to set. Raindrops quickly started falling on the smoking ashes as we started back to the village. Sevim left her eyes among the cooling ashes.

"Either today or tomorrow," Lilith had said, "wait for the return of the waves."

As I opened the door to my house, I looked back one last time. For a while, I watched the skies behind the trees in the distance and said, "Maybe when I wake up tomorrow, you'll be there."

The Sun Also Rises

FROM OUTSIDE, I COULD HEAR the small crackling sounds, the ticking of sleepless bugs in the attic, the rustling of bare branches that hadn't shaken off the storm's fatigue, and the squeaks from the window I'd left open uttered in thin reproach. The window's curtains fluttered in the air. Among the last gusts of the cold wind, I opened my eyes. My ears sharpened to catch that familiar sound I yearned to hear, alert enough to hear the breathing of a snake in hibernation. Yet, I could still sense the void left by the sea. Our shores had not yet revived with the rhythm of the waves. Reluctant to look towards the shore, I got up and changed my clothes, washed my face, and ate breakfast as if not expecting anything. I chewed and swallowed my food slowly.

By noon, my patience had unraveled. I quickly put on my coat and hat, afraid of being late for something unknown, and ran to the shore. My ears had not deceived me. The shore sat like a vast plain of emptiness. The ashes from last night, mixed with rain, had turned to mud. The storm had swept some pebbles and dried moss inland. At the bend at the end of the shallow bay, I saw Fahad. He resembled a small, straight, dark line. It was clear he, too, was waiting. I avoided going over, afraid to face him and hesitant to express my deeply buried despair. On the way back, I caught Sevim's gaze staring at me from her window. My hair stood on end out of old habit. I stayed put and endured the bombardment of her words.

"We've tried in vain," she said with a rasping voice, "I struggled not to lose hope, to give you strength, but I can't escape the gloom that envelops my soul. If the sea doesn't return here soon, you can't escape from me, Azra. You didn't hesitate for a moment to throw the trust I've looked after for years into the fire—I saw it with my own eyes." She unleashed the fury in her eyes upon me.

"It will come!" I emphasized each word. "And when Aegean strikes our shores again, I'll hold you by the hand like a little child and take you to the shore—no escaping. We will swim in it together. It was worth it, I think."

Her face became momentarily contorted by the thought of "swimming." Without a word, she shut the window's curtains in front of me. I laughed out of irritation. Arriving back at my garden without knowing what to think, the bare branches of the fig tree greeted me with their tiny budding leaves. The footsteps of spring were at our door. Another day passed in waiting. When I ran to the shore with the same urgency, I was met with the same empty silence.

"I wonder?" I asked myself. I had neither the courage to complete the question nor an answer to give. Again, Fahad was also waiting at the end of the bay. Just as I was about to return home, at the far end of the void where the sea's horizon once was, I noticed a distinct darkness. It was just visible, like a black thread outlining something. Instead of heading home, my feet chose to run towards Fahad. I was breathless when I reached him.

Pointing to the horizon, I asked, "Do you see her?"

He squinted into the distance, "A spyglass would be very handy now. There should be one at home," he said as he headed for his house. But I couldn't bring myself to leave the shore, stubbornly staring at the dark line. After a while, Fahad returned with it. He looked through the spyglass without speaking. I stared at the same spot, squinting with my eyes.

"It's hard to say anything," he murmured. We sat on the shore until it started to become dark. As evening fell, Fahad stood up, dusting off his knees.

"Excuse me. You should go home too. We won't see anything in the dark."

I went home, put on a couple of layers of clothes for warmth, took a blanket, brewed tea, and headed back for the shore. Nothing could make me stay home. I sat down on some pebbles and lit a small fire, strengthening it with more sticks so the flames wouldn't die down. My eyes were fixed on the desolate sands left by the sea. In the dwindling light of dusk, I observed the horizon for the last time. Night fell. Both my legs and back ached; it felt as though a knife was sticking in it. For relief, I stood up a few times and stretched. Then, I took a short walk along the old shoreline. A timid hedgehog rustled some old, dried-up moss. A white fox came up to me, looked me in the eyes, and then, without lingering, ran back toward the remains of the forest in the distance. Bats flew in the dark, sometimes passing right over my head, startling me. I sat down and dozed off. I awoke when Fahad shook my shoulder, to find the sun had risen. He had found me lying there. The Pearl Seller pointed to the horizon. The blue line had thickened.

"It's coming," he whispered.

We passed his spyglass back and forth between us. He had brought a few treats to eat with coffee and poured it into some cups. We didn't talk much, only to ask short questions like, "When will Aegean hit the shore?" and answer with small guesses. It hadn't occurred to us to tell Sevim. We didn't want her to spill her pessimistic words into the void in front of us. Nevertheless, just before noon, she found us, forcing her ailing legs to run.

"What are you looking at?" Her old eyes were too weak to see the blue line on the horizon. She grabbed the spyglass. "There's a ship passing in the distance."

At first, we didn't believe her.

But after looking again, we noticed what must have been a massive ship, barely visible behind the distant dark mist. It moved slowly; if not observed carefully, one would think it was anchored I tried to examine it with the spyglass for hours. It was undoubtedly made of wood. The white cloth of a sail was unfurled, but I couldn't discern any emblem or symbol on it. The dark portholes offered no clues either.

The mist made it seem more otherworldly, something ancient. From so far away, it was impossible to unravel its mystery. By the afternoon, the ship had disappeared back into the expanse.

The now dark blue line was thickening, taking the shape of a wave. The three of us held our breath, staring at the wave, not daring to speak. We were afraid it might disappear if we did or said something wrong. I couldn't bear to lose the sea again; Aegean was so close to us. The waves have brought me many things since I was little. But this time, it was different. While watching, I saw many things I had lost inside it. My fading dreams, forgotten memories and nightmares were also coming back.

We had no idea what it would bring us this time. None of us had thought to protect ourselves, assuming it would calm down and settle once it arrived at our shores. The excitement of waiting had made us blind. We had forgotten of the pain the sea could inflict and didn't consider her rage or hostility. The wave was getting closer and closer to our shore. What was now a great wave surged toward us faster than we had thought possible, looming before us. It was moving faster and getting larger every second, becoming enormous and mesmerizing. It seemed as tall as Mount Ida. Like a hungry lion, it opened its frothing mouth.

When Fahad had realized the danger and shouted, "Run!" it was too late.

As I turned around, the giant wave crashed over my head, pulling me under. The sound of the world cut out for a moment, and the light disappeared. I was being tossed by the force of the water, and it was impossible to control my body. It felt as if a vast tower had collapsed on top of me. In a panic, I swam with all my strength to reach the surface. Confused, I struggled to keep my head above water. My ears were buzzing, and the salt water burned my eyes. The wave did not just hit our shores; it overflowed into the village. I feared my house was flooded. The sea lifted me up; it was now too deep to touch the ground. I was level with the rooves of the houses along the shore. Fahad and Sevim were nowhere to be seen.

Trying to keep my head above the water, I shouted, "Fahaaaad! Seviiimmm!"

I heard only the sound of the water.

The waters calmed somewhat, and many broken branches and various other debris surfaced. The black moss had spread everywhere, muddying the water. Still, it was not possible to stand firmly on the ground. While swimming aimlessly, a corked bottle passed right in front of me. I grabbed it at once and found a place to steady myself so that I could open it. Inside could be seen a curled piece of paper. I unplugged the stopper and pulled the paper out. Protecting it from getting wet, I raised it high in my hands above my head.

I shouted out loud the two words written, "I won!—Elmados."

I twirled around as if I might find him somewhere near. Water had taken over everywhere. The surrounding black moss chilled me. The more I tried to untangle the moss around my feet, the more entangled it became. Just then, a second giant wave crashed onto the shore. The paper and its bottle I was holding were stripped away.

The moss wrapped around my legs began pulling me under. I tried to resist by grabbing hold of the branches of a passing tree, but the branch broke off in my hand. As the black moss pulled me towards the depths of the sea, I could no longer see the blue sky.

I became submerged under the water, not knowing where the magical moss was taking me.

I thought I would welcome Aegean's return to our shores with joy.

Curse Neptune's thread.

GLOSSARY

börülce: A Mediterranean dish, black-eyed peas

dua: A personal or private prayer

sarma: Tender grape leaves wrapped around a fragrant rice filling with herbs, spices and olive oil

poğaça: A flaky, savory pastry

dersaadet: The gate of happiness, one of the official names of the city of Istanbul, during the Ottoman Empire, particularly in the 19th century.

saadet: Happiness, bliss

sahaf: Second-hand bookseller.

ACKNOWLEDGMENTS

THANK YOU FOR TEACHING ME how to read nature before you left our world, Baba.

I'm deeply grateful to Leni Zumas for her guidance as my honors thesis advisor; her support made my dark clouds disappear. Her office door was always open to me. I'm grateful for your encouragement and belief in me, Professor Leni.

Many thanks to Gabriel Urza for his generous feedback and support, and to Janice Lee for emphasizing the importance of a sentence. I'm so happy to be part of Portland State University, and many thanks to the rest of the faculty and staff in the Creative Writing and English Department.

I'm grateful to Korza Books and Michael Schepps for bringing this book into the world. Many thanks to Jahongir Ashurov for his beautiful miniature artwork, to Yasin Çetin for his wonderful cover design, and Olivia Hammerman for her amazing interior layout.

Since I began publishing short stories, two people have never stopped believing in me and supporting me: Aykut Ertuğrul and Cemal Şakar. Thank you for not forgetting me, even though I was thousands of miles away.

Kerim, if I had not met you, I would never have written in English. I'm grateful we found each other. I'm grateful to my mother for coming to the U.S. whenever I need help. And thank you, Sara and Mina, for always being with me.

GÜZİDE ERTÜRK is a Turkish-American writer currently pursuing an MFA in Creative Writing with a focus on fiction at Portland State University. Her work has appeared in *Kithe Journal*, *The Pointed Circle,* and *The Letter & Line*. Her debut novel, *Kül Ormanı*, was published by Ketebe in 2024 and received the Novel of the Year award from the Writers' Union of Turkey.

GUZIDEERTURK.COM

OTHER TITLES PUBLISHED BY

Korza Books

Is It Just Me or Are We Nailing This? Essays on Bojack Horseman

Published with Antiquated Future

Joshua James Amberson, Timothy Day, Jessica Fonvergne, Lauren Hobson, M.L. Schepps, Jourdain Searles, and Molly E. Simas

Illustrations from Eileen Chavez, Ross Jackson, Naomi Marshall, and Sarah Shay Mirk

Split Aces

M.L. Schepps

Poetry for People: Fifty Years Of Writing

Dixie Lubin

How to Forget Almost Everything

Joshua James Amberson

Altogether Different: A Memoir about Identity, Inheritance and the Raid That Started the Civil War

Brianna Wheeler

The Novel Killings

Kate Shelton

The Last Grand Tour

Michael N. McGregor

Visit KorzaBooks.com or
Follow us on Instagram @Korza_Books

Write to the publisher at
KorzaBooks@gmail.com
for wholesale orders

www.ingramcontent.com/pod-product-compliance
Lightning Source LLC
Chambersburg PA
CBHW050258040926
51005CB00018B/87
* 9 7 8 1 9 5 7 0 2 4 1 2 7 *